"Hey! What're you guys—"

The bedroom door opened and Delia walked in. She stopped with her hand still on the doorknob and her jaw dropped. Ephram flew so far away from Madison he almost fell off the bed.

"What are you guys *doing*?" Delia asked.

Ephram looked at Madison, who paled so quickly he thought she might faint or barf, or both.

"Were you *kissing*?" Delia demanded.

Deny! Deny everything! Ephram's brain screamed.

"Yeah, sweetie, we were," Madison said.

Or you could take that tack, he thought. *Oh, God, now Dad's going to find out.* There was no way around it. He could practically see the wheels in his sister's brain turning. There was definite mileage to be gotten out of this situation. She would have to be an idiot not to see it, and Ephram knew his sister was no idiot.

EVERWOOD

Love Under Wraps

Adapted by Emma Harrison
Based on the television series created by Greg Berlanti, including
the episode "The Burden of Truth," written by Vanessa Taylor; the
episode "Just Like in the Movies," written by Rina Mimoun;
the episode "Unhappy Holidays," written by John E. Pogue;
the episode "Family Dynamics," written by David Hudgins; the
episode "Controlling Interest," written by Michael Green; the
episode "Forget Me Not," written by Wendy Mericle & Patrick
Sean Smith; and the episode "No Sure Thing," written by
Joan Binder Weiss

SIMON SPOTLIGHT ENTERTAINMENT
New York London Toronto Sydney

SSE

SIMON SPOTLIGHT ENTERTAINMENT
An imprint of Simon & Schuster Children's Publishing Division
1230 Avenue of the Americas, New York, New York 10020
Copyright © 2004 Warner Bros. Entertainment Inc.
EVERWOOD and all related characters and elements are trademarks
of and © Warner Bros. Entertainment Inc.
WB SHIELD: ™ & © Warner Bros. Entertainment Inc.
(s04)
All rights reserved, including the right of reproduction in whole or in
part in any form.
SIMON SPOTLIGHT ENTERTAINMENT and related logo are
trademarks of Simon & Schuster, Inc.
Manufactured in the United States of America
First Edition 10 9 8 7 6 5 4 3 2 1
Library of Congress Control Number 2004102536
ISBN 0-689-87107-4

EVERWOOD

Love Under Wraps

PROLOGUE

Ephram Brown was becoming an expert at staring into space. He honed his skills in class, focusing and unfocusing his eyes on the blackboard as his teachers droned on. He honed his skills at the piano, gazing right through the music until the notes danced about on their own. He honed his skills in the shower, at the desk in his room, and while supposedly watching TV. All this space staring wasn't doing much for the fingering skills Will Cleveland was trying to teach him. Or for his history, chemistry, and American lit grades.

But it *was* helping him memorize something:

The lines of Madison's face. The sound of her laugh. The way she had looked on the dance floor at Reverend Keyes's wedding, twirling and giggling with his little sister, Delia. The way her lips had felt against his when he'd kissed her outside the DMV on the day he got his license. The staring was giving him ample time to obsess about the various shades of her hair, the ridiculously cool green of her eyes, and that sexy way she dressed, half rock star, half prep.

It was also giving him plenty of time to formulate a plan. All the good heroes always had a plan, and they usually managed to formulate them in the space of two-to-three comic book frames. Ephram was taking a bit longer than that, but this was important. He had to figure out a way to get a beautiful, cool, older woman like Madison to fall for a junior-in-high-school geek like himself.

That kind of thing took days—weeks, even.

Ephram was sitting on the piano bench in his living room pondering his options when the front door opened and closed. His heart instantly shifted into overdrive and he turned around, expecting to see Madison. Instead his father, Dr. Andrew Brown, walked through the door with Delia in tow. Ephram's face fell. Not only was his dad not Madison, but the man was wearing that smile—that expectant, excited, I've-got-a-plan type of smile—that always seemed to result in Ephram being forced to do something he had less than zero desire to do.

"Hey, Ephram," his father said. "How's the new piece coming?"

Ephram turned to look at the pages on the stand

atop the piano. Right. Music. That was what this thing was supposed to be for.

"Uh . . . good," he said. Then, on second thought, "Actually, not so good. I think I have *a lot* more work to do on it, so I better just stay here for the rest of the afternoon."

"It's going to have to wait until later. We're going out," his dad said. "I have a surprise."

Oh, goody, Ephram thought. "What about Madison?"

"I canceled with her and took the afternoon off," his dad said.

"We're going on a special mission," Delia added with a smile.

And they're in on it together, Ephram thought, dropping the piano's key cover down. *No Madison and a special mission. Can this day get any better?*

"This isn't gonna involve me being laughed at by the general population, is it?" he asked, standing and grabbing his jacket. "'Cause I'm really not in the mood for that today."

His father stepped aside so Ephram could slip past him out the door.

"You never know with me, but I'll try to keep the public humiliation to a minimum," he said.

Maybe if I just jump out at a red light . . . Ephram thought, staring out the passenger-side window of his dad's SUV as it rolled through Everwood proper.

Of course, that never works in the movies, but Dad's pretty slow. . . .

Wherever Ephram's dad was taking him, it was clear on the other side of town. Big stuff if you lived in a small hamlet like Everwood, where everything you needed (or at least all the things Everwood provided) was crammed into a few small blocks.

The car slowed and Ephram looked up at a large painted sign that read USED CARS. His dad was turning into the lot.

No freaking way.

Suddenly Ephram was sitting up straight. His father grinned at him and Delia sat forward excitedly in the front seat.

"Are we doing what I think we're doing?" Ephram asked.

"If you think we're getting you a car, then yes," his father replied, pulling into a space.

"Don't mess with me," Ephram said, glancing around at his prospects. There was a sweet cherry-red Mustang right at the front of the lot. He could just imagine himself pulling up to school in that ride, catching looks from everyone on campus. Forget school—imagine what Madison would think of that baby. A car like that would go a *long* way toward diminishing his geek factor.

"I'm not messing with you, Ephram," his father said. "My son deserves to have his own wheels."

Barely daring to believe his luck, Ephram grinned

4

and scrambled out of the car. If this was some kind of psychotic breakdown his father was having, then he was going to take full advantage of it before the man came back to his senses. Ephram was about to make a beeline for the Stang when an older man in coveralls came walking out from the garage, wiping his hands on an oily rag.

"Hey there, Dr. Brown," he said. "I got her all cleaned up for ya."

"Thanks, Phil," Ephram's father said. "This is my daughter, Delia, and my son, Ephram."

"Hey," Ephram said, so beside himself that it took Phil's words a moment to sink in. "Wait a minute," he said, looking at his dad. "Did you already pick something out?"

"Sure. You didn't think I was going to bring you down here without doing some research first, did you?" his father asked.

Ephram swallowed. This could not be good. Why hadn't he remembered that there was always a downside?

"She's right over here," Phil said, lifting his arm to point down the line of cars, away from the Mustang Ephram was coveting. It was unclear which car he was pointing at, so Ephram followed his dad and Phil, hoping with each successive auto that they would come to a stop. The Jeep Wrangler was nice . . . but they passed that one by. A Ford Focus? Kind of a chick car, but he could make it work. . . . Okay, the Lincoln sedan? Big, but it had a whole Godfather thing going for it. . . .

But his dad and Phil kept walking and walking, passing by every remotely unhideous car and finally stopping behind a boat—a big, huge, silver boat with square lines and a trunk big enough for two baby grands. Both his father and Phil looked at him expectantly. Ephram stared back. They absolutely had to be kidding.

"There she blows," Ephram's father said, beaming.

"You can say that again," Delia said under her breath.

"Emphasis on blows," Ephram added, shoving his hands in his pockets.

"This was my first choice and I didn't even have to go to Denver for it," Ephram's dad said, grinning at the car like it was gold. "Phil just happened to have one in stock. How lucky is that?"

"Yeah," was all Ephram could think to say. He could not be seen in this car. He would be mocked to the ends of the Earth.

"Voted Safest—"

"Boat in the Navy?" Ephram finished for his dad.

". . . Car on the Road in '88 and '89," his father continued, ignoring him, "by the Association of Car Consumers and Retailers."

"She's got heavy steel gauge doors, independent

steel frames," Phil put in. "Weighs about four thousand pounds."

That's comforting, Ephram thought. *Now if someone could just drop it on me and put me out of my misery . . .*

"What do you think of your new wheels, Ephram?" his father asked.

"It's . . . really awesome, you getting me a car, Dad," Ephram said. "It's just—"

"Yeah, yeah," his father said, cutting him off with a wave of his hand. "Hop in. See how she drives. Delia and I can go start the paperwork."

His father started past him and Ephram sensed this was his last chance. Maybe he could get the man to listen to reason. He had been a teenage guy once too, despite all evidence to the contrary.

"It's just, I was kind of thinking . . ." Ephram looked off toward the Mustang, its red exterior gleaming in the sun.

"Don't worry about us," his father said, slapping him on the shoulder. "Go ahead! Hop in! Get acquainted!"

With one last proud-papa grin, his father and Delia were off, leaving Ephram behind with his new albatross. Ephram stared at the car, trying to look for a bright side. There had to be something good about it . . . besides the fact that it could apparently go up against a tank and win. But the more he looked at it, the uglier it got. Did people in the eighties have no aesthetic needs?

"Not what you'd imagined, huh?" Phil asked.

"It's like if you took two of what I imagined, then painted it a color called ugly," Ephram said, taking a couple of tentative steps toward the driver's side door.

"She ain't much to look at, it's true," Phil said. "But don't worry. Your girl will like her."

"I don't have a girl," Ephram said, leaning back against the car. "And I don't think I'll be getting one with this thing. No offense, but this car is a mojo killer and I don't have any to spare."

Phil looked Ephram in the eye. "The girl who's right for you, she'll like this car," he said, all seriousness.

"What, it's like some kind of weed-out?" Ephram asked. "Thanks, but my face pretty much has it covered."

"No. There's a girl, who you like, who likes you," Phil said slowly, never taking his eyes off Ephram's, "and she likes the car."

Ephram blinked. Okay, this guy seemed to be one lug nut short of a full set—whatever constituted a full set of lug nuts.

"A specific girl?" he asked. "Who likes *this* car?"

Ephram tried to imagine Madison pulling up behind this boat in her too-cool vintage Bug and looking impressed. Unfortunately all his mind's eye could conjure was a vision of Madison doubled over laughing.

Phil smiled and lifted a shoulder. "Don't listen to me," he said with a scoff. "What does a guy with grease under his nails know about romance? Here. Hop in," he said, handing Ephram the keys. "Your future awaits."

Ephram popped the door open with a loud creak. The interior smelled of dust and old evergreen-scented air freshener.

"If this is my future," Ephram said, "even my past is starting to look good."

CHAPTER 1

Ephram needed a plan B. For one minute at the car lot, before he saw his four-thousand-pounds-of-steel destiny, his plan A had been to impress Madison with his sweet new wheels. Now that the eyesore was parked in the driveway for all of Everwood to see and mock, he definitely needed a plan B. He lay back on his bed on Sunday afternoon, his arms crooked behind his head, staring up at the ceiling and trying to focus. What could he have that a girl like Madison could possibly want? What did they have in common?

Video games? No. Manga? Nuh-uh. A severe distaste for high school? Maybe, but Madison had been freed from thinking about that three years ago. So what else? What else could he talk to her about?

Ephram turned on his side and spotted the stack

of sheet music Will had sent him home with that morning after their lesson. Suddenly it hit him like a brick to the head. Of course! Music! How could he have missed that? Madison was the lead singer of a garage band that practiced right in Everwood. Ephram was a classical pianist. And, okay, they were two totally different types of music, but if there was one thing Ephram knew, it was that all music was related. And all musicians had an innate bond—a love for their craft, a sense that it was them against the rest of the world.

Ephram had his in.

He sat up straight, his heart pounding with excitement. Now that he knew what to talk to Madison about, he could barely sit still. No more sitting on his butt, obsessing. Ephram would be a man of action. But how?

He happened to know for a fact that Madison's band practiced every Sunday afternoon. It could be the perfect opportunity to show her that he was interested in something she cared about. He could drop in on their session, maybe even give them some input on their songs. The problem was, he had no idea where this session might be taking place.

"Okay, think," Ephram said aloud, standing up. "If you were a garage band, where would you be?"

"In a garage?" Delia said.

Ephram looked up. His little sister was standing

in his doorway, her Avalanche hockey jersey draping down to her knees.

"Ever think about knocking?" Ephram asked.

"The door was open," Delia said with a face that added, *Like, duh*.

"What do you want, Delia?" Ephram asked impatiently. He didn't have time for this. He had to think.

"I'm bored," Delia said. "Wanna help me build my Lego Hogwarts castle?"

"Not right now," Ephram said. "I'm busy."

"You don't look busy," Delia said.

"Well I am," Ephram replied.

"Fine," Delia said, turning away. "Madison would help me."

The second Ephram heard his sister say Madison's name, he realized he had been overlooking one other obvious point. Delia spent more time with Madison these days than with anyone else. It was quite possible that Delia even knew things about Madison. Private things. Things that Ephram would kill to know. His little sister could be a real ally if he played his cards right—which he definitely wasn't doing right now.

"Delia, wait," Ephram said. She turned around again, looking fed up. "Has Madison ever taken you to listen to her band play?"

"Yeah," Delia said. "They totally rock."

Ephram's pulse raced. "Do you think . . . if I

drove you . . . you could find your way to the place where they practice?"

"There are only about ten streets in this town," Delia said. "It's easy." Then she narrowed her eyes at him. "Why?"

"No reason," Ephram said, finding it difficult to act nonchalant when he was so very, very psyched. "I was just thinking about dropping in on their session today, you know, just to see what I think of them."

"I don't know if she'd like that," Delia said, crossing her arms over her chest.

"Why not?"

"They don't want a bunch of groupies hanging around," Delia answered matter-of-factly.

Ephram flushed. "Then why were you allowed to go?"

"I'm not a groupie," Delia said. "I'm a fan. You'd be a groupie."

"Right, well, whatever," Ephram said. "We're going."

"Fine, I'll take you, but on one condition."

"What's that?" Ephram asked.

"When we get home you help me build my castle," Delia replied.

Ephram smiled slightly. "Done."

Delia grinned and ran for her jacket as Ephram grabbed his off the back of his door. That had been about the easiest deal he'd ever had to make.

Little did Delia know, he'd been coveting that Lego set ever since she opened the thing on her birthday.

"This is the biggest car seat I've ever seen."

"Thanks, Delia. That's exactly what I need to hear right now," Ephram said.

"Hey, at least you have a car," Delia said. "I still have to ride my bike." She sat up in her seat to check out the side window. "Turn right, here," she said, just as the corner was flying by.

Ephram slammed on the brakes and made the turn, his monster car straining against the last-minute maneuver. The driver behind him honked angrily and sped up the road.

"I could use a little more advance notice than that," Ephram told his sister.

"Sorry. I can barely see over the dashboard," Delia replied.

Ephram took a deep breath and let it out slowly. It wasn't like he could argue with his sister. She was right. This car was bigger than the freakin' *Titanic*. He could only imagine what Madison and the people in her band would say about it if they saw it. They probably all drove vintage cars like Madison, or tricked-out SUVs, or even spacious old vans for hauling equipment. All much cooler than this monstrosity.

Well, with any luck, they'll never even know this

car is there, Ephram thought. *We'll get in, we'll get out, the* Titanic *will remain out of sight.*

"Okay, make a left and it's the third house on the left," Delia said, sitting up straight with her chin lifted so she could see.

"Got it," Ephram replied.

He turned the corner and his heart plummeted. Standing outside in the driveway of the third house on the left was none other than Madison herself, chatting and laughing with four guys, a couple of whom were smoking. They were lounging around a big blue van with fuzzy dice hanging from the mirror and they all looked up when Ephram slowed down.

"Ephram?" Madison said, her brow creased in confusion.

"You know this guy?" a winner in a black leather jacket asked with a laugh. His friend slapped his shoulder as they cracked up together.

It was Ephram's worst nightmare come true.

Madison approached the car and Ephram rolled down the window—manually. *Just kill me now,* he thought.

"Hey. Hey, Delia," Madison said, leaning in. "What're you guys doing here?"

"Just thought we'd drop by and catch a few songs," Ephram said. "Are you guys done for the day?"

"We're on a break," Madison said, glancing over

her shoulder. She didn't exactly sound welcoming.

"Oh," Ephram said.

"I told you she didn't want any groupies," Delia put in.

Ephram flushed to the color of eggplant. This had to be the worst plan B in the history of mankind.

"You guys can stay if you want to," Madison said, taking pity on him.

"No. That's okay," Ephram said. "You guys are busy—"

"Stay!" Leather Jacket Boy called out, loping over and slinging his arm over Madison's shoulder. "You can tell us all about your . . . what is this thing exactly? A submarine?"

"Jay," Madison said, elbowing the guy away from her. She looked Ephram in the eye and smiled. "Ignore him. He was raised by a pack of wolves. You should stay."

Ephram returned her smile and, buoyed by her defense of him, killed the engine and popped the door open with a loud creak. This sent her friends into another round of hysterics, but Ephram did his best to ignore them. Madison had yet to mock the car. That was all that mattered.

"So, what'd you pay for your ride?" one of the guys asked as Ephram, Delia, and Madison walked around the front of the car. "Five, six bucks?"

"My dad bought it," Delia said, as if that statement would help matters.

"Oooh, a gift from Daddy?" Jay said, laughing. "Think your dad needs a pair of glasses, man. Or maybe that's why he bought it. You can see it coming from miles away."

"Very original," Ephram said. "You write your own stuff or do you farm it out?"

Jay's face fell and he took a swig from the beer he was holding. "Chill, man. Just having a little fun."

Someone can dish it, but can't take it, Ephram thought, trying to squelch a smirk of triumph.

"So, what're you and the munchkin doing here, anyway?" Jay asked, lifting his chin toward Delia, who rolled her eyes at the insult. "You're not hoping to get us to teach you to play or something, are you?"

Ephram opened his mouth to respond, but Madison got there first.

"Actually, Ephram plays piano," she said. "He's pretty good at it, too."

"The best," Delia put in.

Ephram looked at Madison, surprised—and pretty much ready to kiss her feet out of gratitude. Not only was she defending him to her Neanderthal band mates, but Madison had never heard him play a note. Delia must have told her about his music.

"Yeah?" one of the guys asked, eyeing Ephram with a new respect. He pushed his long blond hair behind his ears and blew out a mix of smoke and steam into the cold air. "What kind of music you play?"

"Classical, mostly," Ephram said, shoving his hands in his pockets. "But lately I've been working on some jazz."

"Cool," a third guy said, stubbing out his cigarette under his toe.

"Yeah, cool," Jay said, brushing by Ephram and clapping him on the shoulder as he did. "Maybe one day you'll even get to tour with John Tesh."

He laughed at his own joke and headed inside. Ephram looked at Madison who sighed and lifted a shoulder in apology.

"Nice guy," Ephram said.

"Jay is Jay," Madison replied. "There's no excuse for him sometimes."

"Come on, dude," the bassist said, wrapping his arm around Ephram as he followed after Jay. "We got a new song we're working on. Maybe you can tell us what you think."

Ephram smiled at the affirmation and glanced at Madison.

"Yeah. It's good you dropped by," she said, falling into step with them—on Ephram's side, he was quick to note. "We could use an outside opinion."

Ephram's pulse skipped around as if he had just been asked out on his first date. It wasn't much, but apparently it was all the encouragement his heart needed.

• • •

After three songs and plenty of unwarranted guitar solos by Jay, whose last name seemed to be "I Think I'm Mike McCready," Ephram had concluded exactly three things. First, that Madison was the most amazing singer ever to grace a microphone; second, that his crush was far more serious than he originally thought; and third, Pearl Jam was over, at least as channeled by talentless college-age kids.

The rest of the band was okay. A little sloppy on the changes and off tempo in places, but otherwise fairly talented. If it wasn't for Jay constantly trying to take center stage and outshine the one good thing they had going in Madison, they might actually be bearable.

Madison grabbed the mic with both hands and tipped her head back, holding out a note over the last chord of a slow ballad. Ephram had to grip the edges of the crate he was sitting on to keep from rushing up there and kissing her like she'd never been kissed before. Watching her be so consumed by the music was absolutely intoxicating. Ephram was drunk on pheromones.

"Nice work, guys," Madison said, glancing around at the band. "I think that's it for tonight."

Ephram and Delia stood up. Madison shoved her hands into the back pockets of her jeans as she walked over to them. "Well?" she asked, raising her eyebrows hopefully. "What do you think?"

"What do I think?" Ephram said. "I think you guys are awesome." *And by "you guys," I mean "you,"* he added silently, hoping his total awe didn't come through in his eyes.

"Yeah? You didn't think that last song could use a little work?" she asked.

"Nah. No, not at all," Ephram said. "You guys have a really unique sound." *Again, by "you guys," I would mean "you."*

"Thanks, Ephram. That's really nice to hear," Madison said, biting her bottom lip.

"Hey, Mad. We're gonna go grab a couple of beers," the bassist said as he packed up his gear. "You guys coming?"

"What, are you kidding?" Jay asked, wrapping a cord up around his arm. "This kid needs ID to get milk at school."

Ephram colored instantly, but there wasn't much he could say. Jay, after all, was right. And even if he wasn't, Ephram had Delia with him. She wasn't exactly the best accessory for bar hopping.

"That's okay. We gotta get home anyway," Ephram said quickly, hoping not to prolong the moment.

"Yeah, we have a project to work on," Delia added.

Mental note: Thank Delia later for not telling them we're going home to play Legos.

"Actually, you guys, I'm not really in the mood for drinking," Madison said, turning to the others. "You wanna just go to Sal's Pizza instead? I'm starving."

"I love Sal's!" Delia exclaimed. "Their pizza almost tastes like the pizza in New York."

A couple of the guys laughed, but in a good way, and Madison smiled. "See? Out of the mouths of babes," she said. "Let's go."

"Whatever," Jay said with an elaborate roll of his eyes.

As Madison grabbed up their jackets—hers, Delia's, and Ephram's—Ephram was envisioning feet-kissing for the second time that day. It had to be some kind of record.

The following afternoon Ephram stood in the kitchen, half reading a comic, half watching Madison prep vegetables for that night's dinner, while Delia and his dad sat at the table. Something was up with Madison—Ephram could tell. She was sighing every couple of seconds and mincing the carrots like they'd looked at her funny. This was not a happy girl.

"Something bothering you?" Ephram asked.

"What makes you say that?" Madison asked, bringing a cleaver down on a head of cauliflower with a *thwack*.

"Because I think what you're doing there might be considered maiming in any sane person's cook-book," Ephram replied.

"Jay quit the band," Madison said, chopping down a few more times for emphasis.

"Really?" Ephram asked, his voice nearly cracking out of joy. If he never saw that Jay guy again it would be far too soon.

"Yeah," Madison said, swiping a lock of blond hair away from her face. "I don't know why I'm so upset. This isn't the first time he's walked out. He loves drama."

"Has he always been with the band?" Ephram asked.

"Most of us got together about a year ago, then Jay came in to replace this guy Kip who moved to Oregon to find himself," Madison rambled as she continued to punish the veggies.

"How 1978," Ephram's dad said, looking up from his work.

"If I can't get him to come back—," Madison said.

"You might actually sound okay?" Ephram suggested, sitting down on a kitchen stool and flipping through his comic. "He was so off on that song and then he's all like 'you guys need to change the tempo,' but it was all him. He plays like he's on speed. He's what's bringing you guys down."

Suddenly Madison stopped chopping. The instant absence of noise felt like a death knell to Ephram. It gave him ample time to realize his hideous mistake.

Oh . . . crap.

"Down?" Madison said, the knife hovering above

a stalk of broccoli. "You said we sounded good."

"You did sound good," Ephram said quickly. "I mean . . . I didn't mean . . ."

Oh crap, crap, crap, crap, crap.

"What did you mean, Ephram?" Madison asked. The light was completely and totally gone from her eyes. Yesterday, when he'd said they were good, she had been elated. Now she just looked . . . betrayed.

"Just, he's not as good as you guys, that's all," Ephram said. There. That was diplomatic *and* complimentary.

"How good is that, exactly?" Madison asked.

"So what is this culinary masterpiece you're creating for us, Madison?" Ephram's dad piped in, clearly trying to save his son from being the next vegetable on the chopping block.

"No, it's fine," she said. "Ephram, I want you to tell me the truth."

Ephram looked into her big green eyes and knew there was no way out of this.

"I just think you need a . . . a better guitarist," he said truthfully.

"And?"

"And a better . . . sound . . . and better songs, and—"

Madison dropped the knife with a clang, wiped her hands quickly on her apron, and pulled it off over her head.

So much for honesty. Say something, idiot! Ephram thought. *Say anything!*

"Dr. Brown, take the casserole out in ten minutes and the vegetables should be done by then," Madison said, picking up her bag and her keys. "The rice is on the stove. Somebody check it soon. I'll see you tomorrow."

She walked out and slammed the door behind her. The whole conversation had gone from normal to awful to over in the space of about thirty seconds.

"Your bedside manner might need some work, Ephram," his father said. "You just cleared the room."

Ephram swallowed back a lump of dread. Whatever headway he may have made yesterday had just been obliterated.

"Yeah, I noticed that. Thank you," he said.

"Set the table, doofus," Delia said, slipping out of her chair and walking by him with an accusatory look. "If you can even do that right."

The following afternoon after school, Ephram walked into the house with a whole speech planned. He had worked on it pretty much all day long, resulting in not only a scolding in chemistry class, but ten laps around the gym when he was caught hiding out in the locker room instead of participating in racquetball. Madison and Delia were in the living room playing cards on the floor.

Ephram walked in, hoping for an opening. They ignored him for a good two minutes.

"What are you playing?" he asked finally.

"Spit," Delia said, slapping a card down.

"Go ahead. Tell her how much she sucks at it," Madison said flatly.

Ouch, Ephram thought.

"Listen, what I said last night . . . I didn't mean . . . I mean, I think you're a really good singer and . . ."

Okay, this is not the prepared speech, Ephram told himself. *The prepared speech was much better than this.*

"I just . . . I shouldn't have said anything, okay? I'm sorry," he finished, sounding more defensive than apologetic.

"Was that an apology?" Madison asked, looking up.

"It was supposed to be, yeah."

"Not great," she said.

"It was a rough draft," he lied. "I was gonna polish it up . . . give it to you a little later."

He ventured a smile and something changed in Madison's face. She softened ever so slightly, then looked down and threw out another card.

"It's okay, Ephram. I'm just sensitive about my music because I really want it to be good, you know?" Madison said with a sigh. "I guess I thought—like every other garage band from Podunk, U.S.A.—that I could use it to get out of here."

"I understand that," Ephram said with a shrug.

"But piano—you can take and use it a million different ways," she said. "I need a band, and with Jay gone . . ."

She put her cards down and for the first time since the conversation had started, Delia stopped concentrating on the game. She sat back to wait it out, looking from Ephram to Madison and back. Meanwhile, Ephram's brain was slowly registering that this could be his way back in. This could be the opening he'd been looking for.

"Well, maybe I could help out," Ephram suggested, sitting down on the arm of the couch. "I could sit in on a session or something."

"That's really cool of you to offer, but—"

"No, I could rearrange stuff, whatever," Ephram said.

"He's better than you'd think," Delia put in.

Madison blinked and sat back on her feet. "Are you sure you're up for this?"

Ephram's heart skipped a beat, then raced at the thought of the possibilities. Jamming with Madison, maybe a little alone time working on a song. Plan B was suddenly picking up steam.

"I don't know if it's gonna help, but . . ."

"You know what? We can use all the help we can get," Madison said, slapping her hands on her thighs as she stood. "I'll call the guys. Thanks, Ephram." As she walked out of the room she called back over her shoulder. "I'll be right back, Delia. No cheating!"

Ephram laced his fingers together and smiled, stoked to have come to the rescue of the damsel in distress. He was the hero. Just call him Hero Boy.

Delia groaned and rolled her eyes.

"What?" Ephram asked.

She shook her head as she straightened out her cards. "Boys are so obvious."

Twenty-four hours later, Ephram's fantasy was coming true. He was standing at a keyboard at the back of the garage, playing the simple chord progression while Madison sang her heart out. Every once in a while he made a show of looking down at the keys, just so he wouldn't get caught staring, but it was nearly impossible to take his eyes off her. She was absolutely riveting, and her voice made his heart vibrate.

The song came to a close and Madison looked at the floor. "Is it just me or are we actually getting worse the more we practice?"

"It's just a little off. We'll get it back," Daryl, the blond guy, said.

"All right everyone, take ten," Madison said.

As the other guys moved out of the garage to convene outside, Ephram stayed right where he was. Madison didn't go, so he didn't go. She was the whole point of his being there, after all.

"You still think you can help us?" Madison asked, biting her lip.

"Well, right now you're going like this," Ephram said, playing the chord progression at a low volume. "What if you repeat the four chord after the five before going back to the one? More like that."

He played the new arrangement for her and when she smiled, Ephram's entire body responded.

"Then in the chorus you play the same chords as you have but make the bass line more interesting," Ephram added, on a roll. "Maybe put the G chord over a B bass."

He demonstrated again and watched Madison as she took it in. Her mouth actually opened slightly in surprise, and Ephram had never wanted to kiss her more.

"Why didn't you tell me you were some kind of prodigy?" she asked, sending a dart of pleasure right through his chest.

"Prodigy implies youth while I'm actually an old soul," Ephram said smoothly. "Or at least someone once told me that. So . . . do you like it?" he asked, looking down at his fingers again, which were still playing through the chords.

"Yeah," Madison said with a sweet smile.

Unless Ephram was imagining things, there seemed to be admiration behind her eyes. Real respect and admiration, not *Oh Ephram, you're such a cute little sixteen-year-old* stuff.

Unbelievable. Plan B was working. It was working like a charm.

CHAPTER 2

A few days later Ephram showed up to practice with the band, feeling like the mack daddy of Everwood. He was in a band. An actual band. With Madison, the hottest girl in town, at the mic. Jay was gone and Ephram had rearranged—and improved—half the guy's crappy songs. There was no denying it anymore. Ephram Brown had finally arrived.

He slammed the door of his boat and held his head high as he strode into the garage. Maybe tonight would be his breakthrough night. The more time he spent with Madison lately, the more he could see the change in her eyes. She was attracted to him—he *knew* she was. If she could just get past the age difference thing, which really wasn't that big of a deal anyway, Ephram knew Madison could be his.

At least he hoped and dreamed and prayed she could be.

Ephram stepped into the garage and stopped in his tracks. There, right smack in the middle of the floor, was Jay—off on another one of his pointless guitar solos. The rest of the band, including Madison, stood around smiling and shaking their heads at him in a jovial way. Jay was back. And they were glad.

For a moment Ephram hung by the door, uncertain. What was that tool doing there? Was it for good? And if so, did that mean Ephram was out? There was really no reason for him to stay with the band if they had Jay. They didn't technically *need* a keyboardist.

Ephram turned around to leave before anyone could spot him. They were all so riveted by Jay's Eddie Van Halen stylings they hadn't even noticed when he walked in. He was about two steps from freedom when Madison called his name.

"Ephram!" she shouted, practically skipping over to him. "You're never going to believe it. Jay got us a gig. A real gig at a real bar, with a cover charge and everything."

"That's great," Ephram said, smiling. "So he's back?"

"Yeah. Like I said, he just lives for drama," Madison said.

"Well, then I guess I'll be going," Ephram said, turning again.

Madison grabbed his arm, causing a major spasm in the heart area. "Wait. You don't have to leave just because he's here."

"Yeah, I kinda do," Ephram said.

"Ephram—"

"I rearranged the guy's songs," Ephram said. "And I could be wrong, but I have a feeling he's got one of those egos that can't handle that kind of thing."

Madison smirked and looked away, and Ephram knew he was right. Of course he was right. Jay was cockier than a rooster.

"Just come play with us. He's not an idiot. He'll see that the band is better with you here," Madison said.

Ephram glowed at the compliment. "Yeah?"

"Yeah," she replied, tugging at his arm. "Let's go show him how it's done."

Ephram followed Madison back inside wearing a grin that was never going to wash off. She liked him. She really liked him.

An hour later Ephram was sitting next to Madison on an amp digging into a pizza with the rest of the band. Practice was going well with no more ill-advised guitar solos and a few really tight songs. Maybe Madison was right. Maybe there was room for both him and Jay. Just the fact that she seemed to want him around made him feel as if he could get along with anybody.

"Nice work on 'Acid Emotion,' man," Jay said, glancing at Ephram.

There was a beat in which Ephram was trying to decide if he'd heard correctly. Jay wasn't actually complimenting him, was he? Unsolicited and everything? He glanced at Madison and she smiled, raising her eyebrows.

"Uh . . . thanks," Ephram said.

Jay reached into a cooler and started handing out long-necked bottles of beer. "Beer, Mad?" he asked.

She nodded over a mouthful of pizza and he passed the bottle over.

"Ephram?" he asked, holding one out.

Madison grabbed it from Jay's hand before Ephram could even make a move. Ephram got that sinking feeling in his gut. For five minutes he had almost forgotten his role as youngster in this group.

"I draw the line at actually facilitating illegal activities," Madison explained.

"What? The kid's not twenty-one yet. Who cares?" Jay said. "Did you wait till you were twenty-one?"

"I waited till I was eighteen," Madison replied.

"How old are you?" Jay asked Ephram.

Oh, how he wished he could lie. "Sixteen," he said, wiping his hand on his jeans.

Jay nodded slightly. "I can't even remember before eighteen," he said. "My life didn't start until I moved away from home."

"Guess I'm not actually living then. Good to know," Ephram deadpanned.

"So, what're we going to do about the gig this weekend?" Jay asked, leaning back and resting his shoulders on the windowsill behind him.

"What do you mean?" Ephram asked.

"That's right," Madison said, her face falling. "They're never going to let you into the bar without ID, Ephram."

"Come on," Ephram said with a scoff. Suddenly it seemed as if everyone was looking at him like he was letting them down. It wasn't his fault he was only sixteen! "What, even if I don't drink? I mean, I'm in the band. They've gotta let me in."

"I don't know, man," Daryl said. "The bouncers at the Chute are pretty serious. After that brawl they had there last year they don't mess around."

"Don't look so bummed, Ephram. There will be more gigs," Madison said, putting her hand on his shoulder as she got up.

Yeah. And they'll all be at bars. Call him pessimistic, but Ephram wasn't sure this band was going to last until he was twenty-one.

Madison made her way off to the bathroom and

Ephram dropped his plate with a half-eaten slice of pizza still on it. Sometimes life was completely unfair. Just when he was starting to feel like a real, integral member of the band, he was brutally reminded that he was expendable.

Jay glanced up as Madison slipped through the door, then leaned forward and pulled out his wallet. He slid a card out and handed it to Ephram.

"Here. You can use this," Jay said. "It's my old license. I thought I lost it so I got a new one." He looked Ephram over and tilted his head. "We look enough alike. You can keep it."

Ephram looked down at the ID, totally surprised. "Thanks, man," he said. He thought Jay hated him. Why was he suddenly being so cool?

Jay nodded and leaned back again, taking a slug of his beer. *Huh.* If Jay, of all people, would go to these lengths to get him into the gig, maybe he really *was* an integral part of the band.

Now all he had to do was convince Madison of that fact.

There was something undeniably awesome about being a rock star. Being up on stage above the crowd, the colorful lights flashing in his face, the girls in the crowd cheering and dancing—Ephram had never realized how incredible the feeling was going to be. But it was nothing compared to the fact that the band had decided to use the first song

Ephram had rearranged as their finale. Madison held out the final note and everyone in the bar was on their feet. Not that Ephram could blame them. Madison was worthy of a standing ovation.

"Thank you, everyone!" Madison said into the mic, throwing her arm in the air.

Cheers abounded and Madison jumped down from the stage. Ephram followed right behind while the rest of the band extricated themselves from their instruments. Ephram's heart was pounding with adrenaline and excitement. Their first gig, and everyone totally loved them.

"That was great!" Madison shouted, turning to him as they made their way through the crowd. "That was *so* great!"

"Yeah, it was cool," Ephram said, loving the way she was all lit up from the inside.

"Ephram, you're the best!" Madison said, pausing at the edge of the throng. She turned and threw her arms around him and Ephram hugged her back, surprised. Could this night be any more perfect?

"Your song . . . ," she said.

"It's not my song," Ephram responded, lifting one shoulder as she pulled away. "I just tweaked it a little."

"Your song was the best of all of them," she told him with a grin. "You have to work on 'Joker' with me too."

Ephram smiled. *Anytime, anywhere,* he thought. This was so amazing. A couple of weeks ago he was struggling to find something to talk to her about, and now *she* was asking to spend time with *him*. Ephram was on cloud nine.

"So, what are you doing now?" he asked, pushing his hands into the front pockets of his jeans. "Can I get you a Coke or something?"

Just then Jay walked up behind Madison, grabbed her around the waist and mashed his mouth against hers. For a split second Ephram thought the guy was attacking Madison or something, but then her hand went up and touched his hair and Ephram felt as if the life was being squeezed right out of him. She was kissing him back—big-time.

"That was great, babe," Jay said when they parted. "You coming over?"

"Yeah. After I help these guys pack up," Madison said.

Jay walked off and Ephram felt like he was going to hurl. Madison and *Jay*? But he was such a massive tool!

"Okay, I gotta get going, so I guess I'll see you tomorrow," Madison said.

Unbelievable! How could she act like everything was normal? Like she hadn't just reached into his chest, ripped out his heart, and stomped it into the grimy floor.

"Why didn't you tell me Jay was your boyfriend?" he asked flatly.

"He's not my boyfriend," she said. "We just . . . hang out sometimes."

"Like now? Like when he had his tongue down your throat so long I thought I might have to give you oxygen?" Ephram demanded.

Madison blinked. "Why should I have told you?" she asked.

Okay, she kind of had him there. It wasn't like Ephram and Madison were dating—outside of his dreams, anyway.

"Maybe so I wouldn't have talked about him in front of you," Ephram said, grabbing at the first thing he could think of.

"Jay can be a jerk," Madison said. "I talk about him too."

"It's different," Ephram replied. "Besides, you just should have told me because . . ."

Don't say it. Don't say it!

Madison crossed her arms over her chest and stared at him. "Because what?"

But you like me. You know you do.

Screw it. He had to know.

"Because . . . at the DMV . . . I kissed you," Ephram said. "That meant something."

Madison's brow furrowed and her eyes took on a pitying softness.

"Ephram, maybe it did to you," she said gently.

"It can't mean anything . . . anything real—anything more than what it was."

Ephram wanted to pull his vocal cords right out of his throat. Why did he ever bother putting himself out there?

"You should have told me," he said. "You lied to me."

"I didn't lie to you. I just didn't mention it," Madison said, continuing in that patronizing tone. "We're not friends that way. You're older than your sister but you're still young enough to be someone I look after."

I'm going to die right here, Ephram thought. *Has anyone ever died from a hemorrhaging ego?*

"You have a crush. That's what this is. That's what you have when you're sixteen," she said. "Do you understand?"

"Perfectly," Ephram said, rolling his shoulders back. She was talking to him like he was some little kid, but he wasn't going to let her make him feel like one. Even though he wanted to crawl into a hole somewhere and hide until he was at least twenty-one, he managed to turn around and walk out of the bar with his head up, taking what was left of his dignity with him.

The next day Ephram took out his frustration on his car, waxing it like his life depended on it. He had parked it on the street in front of his house the night before and was now using every muscle available in his upper body to press the rag into the paint, making smaller and smaller circles. No matter how hard he worked, however, he couldn't wax away the image of Madison's pitying eyes, or of Jay sticking his tongue down her throat. It was going to take a lobotomy to fix that problem.

When he heard the putt-putt of an engine turn the corner onto his street, Ephram glanced up. He wasn't sure what to feel when he saw Madison's car coming toward him, but suddenly, he was waxing harder than ever.

The VW pulled up behind Ephram's car and the engine died. Ephram continued to work as Madison got out, slammed the door, and walked over to him. What was she going to say? What could she possibly think she could say to heal the many, many wounds she'd inflicted just hours ago?

"She'll never be much to look at, I'm afraid," she said, running her eyes over the car.

Yeah, that wasn't a good start, Ephram thought.

"Thanks for the encouragement," he said.

"It doesn't matter, though. A car like this, it's not what's on the outside that counts," Madison continued. "See, the thing about big cars . . . they've got lots of room, which is good for friends and movies and road trips. You can fit a whole lot of life into a car like this. That's what makes her cool."

Ephram finally paused in his maniacal waxing.

Madison liked his car. Hadn't Phil said something about a girl he liked, who liked him, who was going to like his car?

"I'm sorry I upset you, Ephram," Madison said. "Especially after you were so cool about the band and everything. I handled it all wrong. I should have told you."

Ephram stood up straight and dropped the rag on top of the hood. "So why didn't you?" he asked.

"'Cause here's the thing," she said. "You're awesome, you know? You've got it all—all the stuff the girls are looking for."

Ephram looked down. This was going nowhere good. "But . . .?" he said.

"But you're sixteen and I work for your dad and I take care of your sister and I'm responsible for you, too," she said.

"No, you're not—"

"Yeah I am," Madison said. "In a way. Can you just see where I'm coming from? You're younger than I am and no matter how mature you are for your age or how much of an old soul you may be, some maturity just comes with time."

Ephram couldn't help smiling slightly over the memory of their "old soul" conversation. She remembered. She actually listened to the things he said and remembered.

"Ephram, you don't even know me."

Ephram looked at her then, and suddenly, the

words came to him. All the things he had been thinking about her, all the ways in which she amazed him. Now was his moment. If he was ever going to pour his heart out, this was his chance.

"I may not know everything about you, but I do know some things," he said. "I know you're the only one who makes my sister think it's okay to be a girl. I know how you feel when you sing because it's how I feel when I play. I know what you want from this Jay guy is for him to really get you, which he never will because the only thing he's interested in getting is himself."

Madison glanced away and Ephram knew he had struck a chord, but he just kept on barreling ahead.

"I know all this stuff about me being too young is just you being afraid, because it's easier for you to say I'm too young than to risk something that's not what you thought you wanted," Ephram said. He took a deep breath. It was now or never. "But most of all I know that ever since I kissed you at the DMV, every time I see you, I want to kiss you again. And I don't know for sure, but I'm pretty certain that you do too."

Ephram took a step closer to her and when she closed her eyes, his heart felt like it was launching into the sky. He touched his lips to hers and this time she responded. She actually kissed him back. It was one of the more perfect moments of Ephram's entire life.

When he pulled away, she looked dazed.

"Thought so," he said.

And then, realizing that one more word from either of them would spoil this movie-worthy moment, Ephram turned and walked into the house, leaving Madison to think about that kiss. Ephram had put his heart on the line and it felt really, *really* cool. It was all he could do to keep himself from laughing aloud in giddy triumph, but he managed.

At least until he got inside.

CHAPTER 3

Ephram pulled his car into the parking lot at County High and tried to ignore the amused stares and outright giggle fits of his fellow students as he drove by. All he wanted to do was just find a space and get into school so he could sit through his day of classes constantly distracted by thoughts of Madison, then go home and endure yet another afternoon of her playing with Delia and acting perfectly normal to him.

Normal. Like that amazing kiss he'd laid on her in front of his house had never happened. What did a guy have to do to get a little attention?

Finally Ephram saw an open spot. He braked so a few cheerleaders could rush in front of the car, and then slid toward the space. Of course Bright Abbott, Rick Martin, Topher Martinson, and a bunch of other seniors were hanging around Topher's Jeep

Cherokee right next to the space. Yet another in a string of unfortunate coincidences that made up the fabric of Ephram's life.

He briefly considered doing another lap around the parking lot, but realized that would only draw more attention to him and the giant-mobile. Body temperature skyrocketing, Ephram bit the bullet and pulled into the spot. Topher nudged Rick, who laughed and elbowed Josh Bryson. Soon there were six varsity-jacketed guys all whooping it up at Ephram's expense.

"Look at Brown's ride, man!" Josh called out as Ephram contorted his body to get out of the car. The door was so big he could barely open it without dinging Topher's Jeep. He slammed the door and walked right past the other guys, ignoring them as usual.

"The Millennium Falcon has landed," Topher called out.

Okay. Ephram couldn't let that one go by. He turned around, shouldering his backpack. "The Millennium Falcon is cool, Martinson," he said. "But I'm sure you'll come up with something better by the final bell."

Topher's face fell. "Good point," he said under his breath.

Bright pushed himself off the hood of the Jeep and jogged up to Ephram as he headed for the front door of the school.

"What do you want?" Ephram asked. He may have thrown Topher's insult back in his face, but that wasn't nearly enough to put him in a good mood.

"Nice to see you, too," Bright said. "I just want to know if Amy's said anything to you."

"About what?" Ephram asked.

"About anything," Bright replied. "She's been acting even more *28 Days Later* lately, if you know what I mean."

"Sadly, I don't," Ephram said, yanking the door to the school open.

"She's like a zombie, man. I figure since you guys are all buddy-buddy—"

"Bright, I'm not gonna spy on your sister," Ephram said, stopping in the hall. "We tried it once before and it backfired big time. Besides, I've got other things on my mind right now, okay?"

Bright pulled his head back far enough to nearly give himself a double chin. "Fine, dude. Chill. Anything I can do?"

"I doubt it," Ephram said, turning down the hall. "But thanks for asking."

With that, Ephram walked off to commence his day of half-assed note taking and constant Madison obsessing. He twirled the lock on his locker, trying to recall if he'd done the homework for trig class, when a peal of female laughter down the hallway caught his attention—along with almost everyone else in a one-mile radius. Ephram looked up to find Bright picking Tanya Sugarbaker up under her butt, slinging her over his shoulder, and spinning her around while four other girls looked on and laughed. Tanya shrieked, beating Bright's back with her fists.

"Put me down! Put me down!" she shrieked, not sounding at all like she wanted to be put down.

Bright obliged, however, and Tanya tossed her hair back and smiled up at him, flushed and happy. A cloud must have shifted outside, because at that moment a beam of sunlight bathed Bright and his little crowd of admirers in its golden warmth. Ephram was not immune to the cinematic symbolism.

How could he have been so stupid? Of course there was something Bright could do to help him. Bright was exactly the person he needed.

"You and me. Friday night. Everwood Video Store," Bright said, following Ephram down the comedy aisle inside the small, cozy shop. "How did I get here?"

"It's called slumming," Ephram said, picking up a box at random and replacing it. The Everwood Video Store was not exactly Blockbuster. It had half the titles and only one copy of each film. Plus they had only upgraded to DVD about five minutes before Ephram had arrived in Colorado. But like any other small town in the U.S. of A., it was Everwood's main weekend attraction for the under-twenty-one set, and plenty of the above-twenty-ones, as well.

"How about this?" Bright asked.

Ephram turned, took one look at the boobali-cious girls on the cover of the DVD his friend was holding, and shook his head.

"No."

"Dude, look how much fun they're having," Bright said. "With the bikinis and the beach balls . . . we could be having that much fun." He pointed at the curviest blonde in the picture. "You see her? That top comes *off*."

Ephram wondered how many times Bright had seen *Beach Party Ten*, but decided he didn't really want to know.

"I'm not in the mood to sit through two hours of guys who look like you making out with girls who look like that," Ephram said, continuing to browse. "Not after I've been rejected twice by a girl who's even hotter than some stupid bikini model."

Ephram paused in front of an Academy Award-winners section and grabbed a title. "Here. Let's just get *The Pianist*."

"No way. Just 'cause you got the Heismann doesn't mean I have to rent some lame piano movie," Bright said, taking the movie out of his hands and slapping it back onto the shelf.

Ephram glanced at Bright. Half the time he had no idea what this kid was talking about.

"It's not just about piano," Ephram protested. "It's also about the Holocaust."

"Yeah. That's a selling point," Bright scoffed.

"Get whatever you want," Ephram said as a group of preteen girls squeezed by him. "I don't care anyway."

Bright looked at him with a pitying expression that Ephram was growing all too used to seeing.

"All right, huddle up," Bright said, waving his hand in Ephram's direction. Ephram just looked at him.

"That means come *here*," Bright said, rolling his eyes. "Man, it's like working with raw clay." Ephram rolled his own eyes in response and took a step toward Bright. "You're obviously stuck on this chick, so you need a game plan."

"Which is where you come in," Ephram said.

"Exactly. Now, you went the Way of the Wuss," Bright told him. "The 'stick a boombox in the air, lay your heart on the line' Cusack crap. That bit is tired. Bottom line, you don't want to be living inside some dippy romantic comedy."

A romantic comedy actually didn't sound so bad to Ephram. After all, the guy always ended up with the girl in the end, right?

Bright pulled an action movie off the shelf and held it up. The cover was all bisceps bulging, lips snarling, girl swooning, while stuff exploded in the background.

"You want to be living the life of an action star. Like the Rock," Bright said. "Saving Japan by day and the ladies by night."

Ephram squinted at the picture. "That man's bicep is twice the size of my entire body. I'm leaving now—"

"Forget the Rock," Bright said, grabbing his shoulder with a strong grip; Bright's strength never ceased to surprise Ephram. "We'll work with what you have. And what *you* have is that mysterious vibe. That Joaquin Phoenix, 'I could go postal on your ass at any minute' kind of thing. You gotta keep her guessing."

Ephram was intrigued. Joaquin Phoenix? He could be down with that. "How do I do that?" he asked.

"By ignoring her," Bright said.

"Ignore her," Ephram repeated, stumped. "That's the game plan?" The girl was practically ignoring him at the moment, so it didn't seem like much of a strategy.

"It's perfect. Right now she's expecting you to be all 'Hey! Sorry about copping a feel the other day—'"

Ephram reddened. "I did not cop a feel!" he whispered, looking around.

"But if you ignore her, you maintain your position

of power by keeping her totally confused about what's going on in your head," Bright continued, "which only makes you more intriguing. Nothing keeps a girl around like the possibility that you might not want her there."

Ephram mulled it over and realized that this could, quite possibly, be true. The expression "You always want what you can't have" was an expression for a reason, right? What was disturbing was that Bright, who knew almost nothing in the grand scheme of things, knew this. And used it on unsuspecting women.

"That actually makes sense," he said finally. "It's completely evil, but it makes sense."

Bright grinned and took the action movie toward the register. "Don't hate the player," he said over his shoulder. "Hate the game."

A few days later Ephram came home from school and saw Madison's car parked out front. He instantly tensed up and started repeating Bright's advice in his head like a mantra.

Just ignore her. Be Joaquin. Just ignore her. Be Joaquin.

Of course when he opened the back door and saw Madison standing there, helping Delia fill up the goody bags for her upcoming birthday party, looking all beautiful, the advice seemed almost impossible to put into action.

"Hey," Madison said with a smile.

Ephram swallowed hard and closed the door. *Just ignore her. Be Joaquin.*

He nodded a hello. Very smooth. Very playa.

"I thought maybe we'd do a pizza tonight," Madison said, dropping a mini-bag of M&Ms into one of the plastic pouches. "Would that be cool with you, Ephram?"

Just be cool, Ephram thought, and shrugged in response. *Be Joaquin.*

"Did you lose your voice or something?" Delia asked.

Ephram flushed. The ignoring plan became a little more difficult when a nosy sister was involved. He glanced at Madison who smiled slightly.

Oh, God. Does she know I'm being Joaquin? Ephram thought, panicking.

"Or else I found this recipe in *Jane* magazine that I could try out," she suggested. "I don't mind cooking if you'd rather."

She was acting like she was his mother or something. *What do you want for dinner, sweetie? If you eat all your vegetables, you can have dessert!*

"I don't care," Ephram said, sounding a bit harsh. "Whatever."

"Ephram—"

Before she could finish whatever she was going to say, her cell phone trilled. Madison yanked the silver flip phone out of her back pocket and checked the caller ID. Ephram saw her shoulders tense up and her entire face changed. Something was going on.

She flipped the phone open and turned away from him, tucking her hair behind her ear. "What's up?" she said into the phone. "I'm still at work, but I'm almost done." There was a pause and she turned farther away. "Oh, please. Look, Jay—"

Ephram's stomach hurled itself off the high dive when he heard Jay's name. Was she still dating that loser? Was that why she'd been walking around pretending like nothing had happened between them?

"If you don't want to go with me, that's fine," Madison said, her voice tight. "That's not what I said. You're twisting my words around again. . . ."

Finally she seemed to decide this wasn't a conversation she wanted to have with an audience and she turned around and headed out the back door onto the porch. Ephram strained to hear what she was saying, but her voice was too muffled.

"If you're gonna sit here, help," Delia said.

"Shhhhh," Ephram told her, leaning toward the door. Delia shot him a look, so he picked up some candy and tossed it into one of the bags.

"Hey! One Gobstopper per bag!" Delia scolded him. "One!"

Madison walked in and closed the door with a bang, shoving her cell phone back into her pocket. She was clearly not a happy camper. Ephram studied her, waiting for her to give him some kind of clue as to what was going on. Why did she stay with a guy who made her so obviously unhappy?

"Are you guys done with those?" she asked, distracted.

"Finished. Did you just have a fight?" Delia asked.

Okay, so maybe a nosy sister was a *good* thing to have around.

"No. That was just—"

"Jay," Ephram said aloud without meaning to. Madison and Delia looked at him and he flushed. "Birds," he said quickly to Delia. "Jaybirds would be a good thing to have at your party."

Delia looked at him like he'd lost his mind, which he may have done.

"What?"

"It's a type of bird. And birds sing. Which thematically links in with your whole karaoke concept," Ephram said quickly. "Just a thought."

Then, with Madison staring at him blankly, he got out of there as fast as his legs would carry him.

The Saturday of Delia's party arrived and Madison came over to help Delia with last-minute details. Realizing it would be much easier to ignore Madison if he didn't actually have to see her, Ephram spent most of the day locked up in his room. He turned on the stereo at one point, but when he realized that it pretty much obliterated his ability to hear Madison's every move, he turned it off and decided that reading would be a much more useful way to spend his time.

He could hear her walking around in the kitchen, opening and closing cabinets, calling out to Delia when she had a question. Even through the floor he could hear there was something different in her voice. Something strained—like she was trying to sound happy and party-day psyched, but it was taking a lot of effort.

I should go down there and see what's wrong, Ephram thought, sitting up on his bed. *Maybe she needs somebody to talk to.*

He swung his legs over the side of the bed and paused. No. Bad idea. Going down there and asking her if she was okay would definitely be going against the plan. And right now the plan was the only thing he had going for him.

"I'm putting the cupcakes in the oven, Delia," Madison called out. "That's thirty-five minutes to icing time."

"Cool!" Delia replied.

Ephram sighed. Maybe she wasn't upset. Maybe he was just imagining the tone. But he *so* wanted to see if she was okay.

This is ridiculous. How do you just ignore someone you care about? Ephram thought. He pushed himself up and barreled down the stairs and into the living room. The second he saw Madison in the kitchen, however, he chickened out. What if she didn't *want* to talk to him? And what would Bright say if he knew what Ephram was considering?

Probably nothing. He'd probably just smack Ephram in the back of the head.

Okay, now he was hovering and he looked like a moron. Time to start acting like this was actually his house. He quickly dropped down on the couch next to Delia, who was tying ribbons onto her goody bags, then slumped down as far as possible so Madison wouldn't be able to see or hear him.

"What's wrong with you?" Delia asked, looking at him with that dubious expression she'd been gracing him with so often lately.

"Nothing. But something's wrong with Madison," Ephram whispered. "I think she's upset."

"I know," Delia said. "I'm ten, not stupid."

"So why don't you go talk to her?" Ephram suggested, feeling only slightly guilty over using his little sister as a pawn in his sordid romantic life. "Make her feel better?"

"How am I supposed to do that?" Delia asked.

"Tell her you like her sweater. Or her hair," Ephram suggested. "Either one."

"Why don't you tell her?"

"Because she'd be happier if it came from you," Ephram said quickly.

"Why would she—"

"Just do it," Ephram snapped.

Delia stood up and rolled her eyes. "Fine, but if you get any weirder, we're gonna have to send you away."

She walked into the kitchen and Ephram pushed himself up slightly on the couch to expose one ear to the conversation. He crossed his arms and legs and tried to look natural, which—with the head-tilt—was rather painful, but he held the position. He had to hear what was going on without looking like he cared.

"Hi, Madison," Delia said. "I like your sweater."

"Thanks, Delia," Madison said, sounding tired.

There was a moment of total silence and Ephram hazarded a glance over his shoulder. Delia widened her eyes at him like, *What now?* He waved both hands at her to get her to keep trying.

"And you don't have any pimples, either," Delia said.

Ephram stifled a groan and sat back down. Maybe Delia wasn't the best person for this job.

"Thanks," Madison said. "I'm sorry I've been such a bummer all day. I'm kind of in a rotten mood."

"Why?" Delia asked.

"My plans for tonight fell through," Madison explained. "I was supposed to have this date, but instead we decided to break up. It's just sucky, that's all."

Break up?! They broke up?! This is incredible!
Ephram thought.

"Well, if you don't have anything to do tonight,
you should come to my slumber party!" Delia said
excitedly. "You'd have a great time."

*Omigod! Did she just say what I think she just
said?* Ephram thought, panicking. He could not
have Madison in his house all night, witnessing the
ridiculousness that was his sister and her friends.
Abort, Delia! he thought. *Abort!*

"I don't know, sweetie," Madison said.

Please say no, please say no, please say . . .

"C'mon! There's gonna be karaoke and pizza and
you have to meet my best friend," Delia begged.
"She's really cool. Please?"

"You know what? That does sound like fun,"
Madison said finally. "I'd love to come to your
slumber party, Delia. Thank you."

Oh God. Why do I bother? Ephram thought,
hanging his head. He looked over his shoulder and
Delia grinned, flashing him a double thumbs up.
In her little mind she'd succeeded on her cheer-up
mission. Unfortunately, in the process, she'd pretty
much killed her brother.

That night Ephram experienced life in the ninth
circle of hell. He sat on the couch in his living
room, sandwiched between his father and Madison,
watching Bright as he sang his tenth song into the

karaoke mic. This time he'd gone for a real classic: Destiny's Child's "Independent Women." Around him, a dozen ten-year-olds waved their hands, danced, and stared up at him like he was a god. Meanwhile all Ephram could do was try to sit far enough away from Madison to keep from touching her while somehow not cuddling into his father like a five-year-old. He was sweating from the exertion.

"All the women, independent!" Bright sang.

"Throw your hands up at me!" the girls responded.

Bright had insisted he come to the party the second he heard Madison was going to be there. He told Ephram he needed a wingman—someone to keep him on the straight and narrow so he wouldn't mess up the plan. Listening to his tone-deaf friend try to sing, Ephram was starting to regret he'd spoken to Bright—ever.

Madison was clearly upset over her breakup with Jay. Even though Ephram was happy that the two of them were over, his heart went out to her. It killed him, seeing her sad. And the way she was putting on a happy-go-lucky front for Delia just made him admire her more. Part of Ephram wanted to hang tough and continue to go along with Bright's plan, but wasn't ignoring the girl when she was feeling so awful kind of like cruel and unusual punishment?

"Girl, I didn't know you could get down like that!" Bright sang. *"Charlie how your angels get down like that!"*

Actually, that *is cruel and unusual punishment,* Ephram thought, glancing at Madison from the corner of his eye. The poor girl had no idea what she was getting herself into when she had accepted Delia's invitation.

"I think I need another soda," Ephram's dad said, pushing himself up.

Ephram's heart hit his throat. If his dad got up, that left him and Madison alone on the couch. Definitely not a good idea.

"You have a full can right here," Ephram pointed out.

"Yes, but if I get another one, I can escape to the kitchen for a whole five minutes," his dad replied with a conspiratorial smile.

"You're smarter than you look," Ephram told him.

Ephram glanced over at Madison and she was looking right at him. His heart thumped and he retrained his attention at Bright. This was total torture.

"Don't take this the wrong way, but your friend's a little weird," Madison said.

"Let's just pray he's done with the ballad portion of the evening," Ephram replied.

Oops. That wasn't exactly ignoring. But he wasn't fawning all over her either. Simply a comment at

Bright's expense. That couldn't be that bad, right?

"So why does it seem like we haven't talked in forever?" Madison asked, turning toward him.

Ephram opened his mouth to reply, but before he had a chance Bright plopped down right between them on the couch, still holding the microphone. He was so big that wedging himself into the spot meant practically sitting his legs on top of theirs.

"Dude, I feel a duet comin' on," he said to Ephram. "How do you feel about Peabo and Celine? You can be Peabo. . . ."

"I don't think so," Ephram replied.

"No problem. Plenty to choose from," Bright replied. He looked at Madison with an almost offended expression. "Could you move down a little? You're, like, all in my space here."

Madison glanced at Ephram and he knew she was expecting him to say something. After all, Bright *was* being ridiculous, but Ephram couldn't do anything without veering from the plan. He was stuck. So he looked away.

"Yeah. Sure," Madison said, standing.

She walked off and Ephram watched her go, feeling awful. She'd come here in a lame attempt to cheer herself up and now the one person in the room that could reasonably be called her friend—Ephram himself—was treating her like dirt. This was so not him.

"That was real smooth," he said to Bright.

"Told you," Bright said, oblivious to Ephram's sarcastic tone. "Wingman."

All night, even though he was "ignoring" her, Ephram knew exactly where Madison was. He was aware when she moved from one room to another and went on high alert every time her cell phone trilled. At one point she went outside to talk on the phone and he almost fell off a stool trying to hear her side of the conversation. She never came back inside.

After the girls had all dozed off in their sleeping bags on the living room floor, Bright had crashed on Ephram's bed, and his dad had disappeared somewhere, he finally had a chance to go outside and see if she was okay. Her car was still in the driveway, so he knew she hadn't taken off. What had she been doing out there for the last half hour?

Ephram opened the back door and paused. Madison was sitting on the porch with a blanket draped over her legs, staring out into the driving rain. Ephram's heart started to pound. She looked so down and alone. What the hell had he been thinking following Bright's advice?

He stepped out into the cold, closed the door, and sat down next to her, staring straight ahead. Madison didn't move. It was like neither was acknowledging the other's existence, but they each knew that the other was hyperaware of the awkwardness between them.

"I thought you were ignoring me," Madison said.

Ephram flushed and looked down at the step. "What gave it away?"

She glanced at him then, sitting there in his short-sleeved T-shirt, his breath making steam in the frigid night air. "You must be freezing."

"I'm fine," Ephram said. "You want to talk about it?"

"Not really."

"You sure?" Ephram said. "I'm a good listener."

He wasn't entirely certain he wanted to hear her tale of woe and heartache—how devastated she was over losing Jay. But he knew he wanted to be there for her. And if that meant hearing about how much she cared about the guy, then he could handle it.

Madison looked at him, her hair tumbling over one shoulder, and smiled. "I know you are," she said.

"So what did he do?" Ephram asked. "Was it just standard obnoxious behavior, or what?"

Madison smiled, took a deep breath, and turned to face Ephram. He felt as if something big was coming, but he had no idea what it was going to be.

"Jay broke up with me because he thought . . .

well, he thought I didn't feel about him the way he feels about me," Madison said. "And he wasn't wrong."

Ephram couldn't have been more shocked if Bright had burst out of the house at that moment wearing nothing but Delia's Powerpuff Girls pajamas. *Jay* liked *Madison* more than *Madison* liked *Jay?* He had thought they were in one of those jackass-guy-doesn't-appreciate-his-perfect-girl relationships.

"Oh, well . . ." Ephram was at a total loss for words. "You know. That happens."

"Yeah. It does. But then he accused me of liking somebody else," Madison said.

"Somebody else?" Ephram said, his heart turning over about a thousand times. He couldn't believe this. There was *more* competition? Someone other than Jay? "Oh, God. Please don't tell me it's the drummer."

"No. It's not the drummer," Madison said with a laugh.

"Oh. Good," Ephram said. Then he realized that her words implied that Jay was right. It may not be the drummer, but there *was* someone. "But there is someone else," he said, letting his thoughts tumble out. He turned away, fighting to keep his imagination from conjuring up an image of the perfect Adonis Madison was interested in now.

"I didn't think there was. I mean, when Jay said

it, I told him he was crazy," Madison said. "Me and that other guy are just friends. But then I realized that I get excited every time I know I'm about to see this particular friend. My stomach gets all fluttery when he walks in the room."

Okay, this may very well be the worst moment of my life, Ephram thought, trying not to look as distressed as he felt.

"And I don't exactly know when that changed, exactly," Madison continued. "It might have been the first time I saw him play music."

She paused and Ephram felt as if the world stopped spinning for just a moment. Wait a minute. She couldn't be talking about *him,* could she? He looked up at her, a torturous mixture of hope, fear, and surprise, and saw it in her eyes. She did like him! He'd been right all along! This was actually the most *perfect* moment of his life.

"Or maybe it was when he told me how he felt about me," Madison said. "I've never had anyone talk to me like that before. It was as if he was ten years older than me instead of four years younger. But the clincher was when he kissed me. In that moment . . . I don't know . . . I just came undone."

Ephram exhaled a breath he hadn't realized he was holding. He couldn't remember ever having felt this hopeful, this excited. What was he supposed to say to a speech like that?

"Well, unfortunately your taste in guys leaves a

little something to be desired," he said, going for the self-deprecating joke as usual. Madison smiled slightly and Ephram couldn't stop himself from grinning as well. "But if this is what your gut's telling you to do, I think you should go for it."

Madison's smile widened and she leaned forward and kissed Ephram—for real. The first kiss that was all her. And as Ephram closed his eyes and kissed her back, the giddy little voice in his mind kept repeating one little word.

Madison. Madison, Madison, Madison.

He couldn't imagine ever wanting anything, or anyone, more.

CHAPTER 4

Amy Abbott sat back in her chair in the cafeteria on Monday and watched as her brother Bright and Ephram Brown made their way over to a table together. When had those two become close enough to be lunch buddies? Was Amy missing something here?

"And then Bobby told me I have the most beautiful eyes he's ever seen, which *has* to be an exaggeration, but still, you know, it was nice," Laynie Hart rambled on across the table. Amy only tuned in to every other word. She'd heard enough about Laynie's new boyfriend to fill an entire diary. And none of it was all that interesting.

Actually, I've been missing a lot *of things lately,* Amy realized, watching her former friends Page and Kayla gab and laugh as they exited the lunch line. The two of them walked over to the table Amy used to share with them every day—used to also share with Bright and Colin. When had Amy stopped sitting there? When, for that matter, had she completely stopped talking to Page and Kayla? And when had she stopped talking to Ephram and Bright enough to not know they were so simpatico?

Lately it felt like Amy had become a spectator of her own life. Maybe it was the antidepressants. Could drugs that were supposed to make you happy make you feel this . . . detached? Clearly they weren't having the same numbing effect on Laynie.

"So then he told me about this party this weekend," Laynie was saying now, turning her water bottle around and around. "It's at his friend Mark's house, whose parents are going to be away. We have to go."

"*Laynie,*" Amy said with a bit of exasperation in her voice. The very thought of going to another one of her friend's many parties made her feel exhausted.

"I know what you're going to say, but it won't be like ECC," Laynie said. "Bobby's friends are totally cool. You'll love them."

"No. I won't," Amy said, slumping now.

Laynie blinked and a little crease appeared over her nose. "What do you mean, you won't? How can you say that about people you haven't even met?"

Behind Laynie, Kayla passed Page a CD and

they leaned in to read the list of songs together as Page munched on a carrot stick. They looked like they were having such a good time. At least they were talking about something other than boys and parties—the only two conversation topics Laynie ever tapped into these days. Why had she stopped hanging out with them? Was it just because of Colin? Suddenly Amy wanted her friends back. She wanted to talk to someone other than peppy, kiss-and-tell, party-animal Laynie.

"Look, I'm just a little tired of going to all these boring house parties," Amy told her. "Nothing interesting ever happens at them."

Laynie's expression darkened further, as if Amy had personally insulted her. "Well maybe that's because you never talk to anyone. You stand up against the wall for three hours, then go home. You're the boring one."

The second Laynie said it, something behind her eyes changed, like she realized she had stepped over some line. Amy felt it too, and it was enough to push her to her feet.

"Tell me how you really feel," she said before walking off toward the bathroom. She had to get away for a couple of minutes. Sometimes being with Laynie was just too high-intensity for Amy. Too much activity, too much talk, too much volume— just too much.

She pushed open the heavy bathroom door and

found two senior girls standing at the mirror applying lip gloss. They both looked at her like she was wearing last season's jeans. Amy ducked her head and slipped into one of the stalls. She dropped her bag, sat down on top of the toilet, and pulled her feet up.

Deep breaths. Just take a few long, deep breaths, she told herself, wrapping her arms around her legs. She rested her head on her knees and listened as the girls packed up their stuff and walked out.

What am I doing in here? Amy wondered morosely, looking down at the grimy floor. *When did I become the girl that hides out in the bathroom at lunch?*

This cafeteria break was certainly bringing up a lot of questions. Maybe she should be proactive— decide not to be the loser she had apparently become. Maybe she should walk right back out there, sit down with Kayla and Page, and find out what music they were listening to. It would probably be a lot healthier than staying in hermit mode.

Amy was about to relinquish her stall when the door opened again. Two voices filled the room and their words made her hand recoil from the silver lock.

"Did you *see* what Amy was wearing today?" one of the girls asked.

"I know! Is she hoping to single-handedly revive the grunge look?" the other replied.

"Like anyone wants to Bogart her fashion any-more," the first girl replied. "She's a total space case and the wardrobe reflects it."

Amy sat back down on the toilet seat—hard. It was Page and Kayla, the very "friends" she was about to go visit with in the caf. They were talking about her like she was some kind of social leper. At some point in her life, Amy might have walked out of the stall and confronted them, but just then she was too stunned. People were talking about her? *Friends* were talking about her? This was totally surreal.

"If Colin were still alive, he would not be dating her now, I'll tell you that much," Kayla said, causing tears to spring instantly to Amy's eyes.

"I know, right?" Page replied. Then she sighed wistfully. "He was so yum."

God! Do they even hear themselves? Amy thought, struggling to keep from making a noise. *They can't. They can't know how awful they sound.*

"Come on. I wanna finish my salad before the bell," Kayla said.

In two seconds they were gone, and Amy's feet hit the floor like a couple of bricks. She couldn't believe everything she had just overheard—couldn't believe that she and Colin had ever been friends with people like that. Laynie was a little boy crazy, but she would never talk about a friend that way. Never in a million years.

Which was good—because apparently, Laynie was all Amy had left.

That weekend, at Laynie's boyfriend Bobby's best friend Mark's parentless party, Amy found herself doing exactly what Laynie had predicted she would be doing: standing against the wall, checking her watch, talking to no one. Laynie had gone off to make out with Bobby the second they'd arrived and hadn't been seen or heard from since. Amy couldn't figure out why it was so important to Laynie that she come to these things if she was just going to desert her once they got there. It was like she needed moral support to walk through the door and then Amy was magically removed from her radar the second Bobby's blip showed up.

Amy took a sip of her Coke, sighed, and leaned her head back until it hit the doorjamb behind her. A couple of people were making out on the sofa in front of her while a girl stood against the far wall holding court with three guys, each of whom was trying to out-flirt the others. A bunch of boys were having a chug contest in the corner and one of them crushed a can against a table, then hurled it at the wall.

Big fun.

Amy turned to check out another angle and see if she could find anything more intriguing to watch. That was when she saw Tommy Callahan watching her from across the foyer.

Quickly Amy glanced away and took another sip of her drink. She had flirted briefly with Tommy at the pharmacy the other day—back when he was a nameless register boy—but later she had found out who he was and heard the rumors. Tommy had been addicted to crystal meth and had even gone to rehab for it. Laynie had told her he was bad news—something about trying to burn down his locker at County back when he went there—and Amy hadn't thought about him since. Yet there he was, blatantly staring at her at Bobby's best friend Mark's parentless party.

"Hey," he said in her general direction.

Amy glanced up again and confirmed he was, in fact, talking to her. "Hey," she replied.

"I'm Tommy," he said, pushing his hands into the front pockets of his quite flattering, perfectly broken-in jeans. His blue eyes swept over her in an appreciative, yet nonthreatening way, and she could tell he remembered her from their exchange at the pharmacy.

"Yeah. I know who you are," Amy said with a touch of superiority.

"You probably shouldn't drink that," he said as if he didn't remotely notice the tone. "Alcohol doesn't mix well with . . . uh . . . you could get really sick."

"Yeah, I know," Amy replied quickly, glad he hadn't announced to the room that she was on Zoloft, which he only knew because she had purchased it from him. "It's soda and it's actually none of your business, so—"

"Sorry. I didn't mean to be an ass," Tommy replied, interrupting her. "I only said something 'cause I usually don't know anything worth anything, so when I do, I have to say it."

"It's good to know that your expertise lies in knowing what kind of drugs and alcohol don't mix," Amy said. "That's great."

He let the insult slide as well. He even smiled slightly. "What's your name?"

This is going nowhere good, Amy thought. But she said, "Amy."

"So, Amy. Do you maybe want to continue this conversation somewhere that doesn't have a keg?" he asked.

He smiled in an inviting way and Amy found herself smiling back. He wasn't *so* scary. In fact, when he looked at her like that he was actually kind of cute. But still, with words like "addict," "meth," and "fire" floating through her mind, she didn't feel entirely comfortable.

"I don't think that's such a good idea," Amy said.

"Why? You afraid you're gonna miss out on this incredible party?" he asked, slowly approaching her across the foyer.

Amy stood up straighter. "Yeah, right."

"So what's the worst thing that could happen?" he asked.

Murder, rape, drug use, you name it, Amy thought. But she didn't *feel* it. What she felt was that Tommy seemed interesting, and even nice. And that not much could be worse than this lame-ass party.

"I don't know—you could be boring," she joked.

Tommy laughed and the admiration that was already evident in his eyes seemed to deepen. Amy realized with a pang that no one had looked at her like that in quite a while.

"I'll tell you what. If I'm more boring than this party, I'll give you something of mine to keep," he said, reaching back into his pocket. "How 'bout my cell phone?" he said, offering up a slick silver number.

Amy looked at Tommy and her heart responded with something that could only be described as excitement. At least it was as close to excitement as Amy had come since Colin died. Tommy was definitely mysterious, and there was definitely potential for trouble here, but who cared? Maybe it was time for the perfect Amy Abbott to do something a little rash.

She reached out, took the phone, and pretended to be appraising it.

"Does it come with a headset?" she asked.

Tommy smiled, knowing he had her, and Amy

dropped her cup and followed him to the door. Part of her knew it might be the dumbest thing she had ever done—leaving a party with a perfect stranger, a stranger with a rep, no less—but she didn't care. She had to trust her instincts. And her instincts were telling her she was about to have some actual fun.

If Laynie could see me now . . . Amy thought as she and Tommy flipped through the musty old albums at the used record store near the edge of town. The place had been there forever and Amy had never seen a single soul walk though its door. The posters in the window were so sun-faded, a person could barely make out their graphics. Laynie thought Amy was so predictable, yet here she was, standing in a place in Everwood she had never set foot inside of before. After sixteen years in this rinky-dink town, it seemed impossible that such a place existed.

"This guy is my hero," Tommy said, pulling out a Leonard Cohen album and slipping it free of its protective plastic covering. "Poet-turned-songwriter-turned-Buddhist. Went from living a totally indulgent musician's lifestyle that took him all over the world to monking out on Mount Baldy. 'Chelsea Hotel' is just about the most amazing song ever written," he said. "You *need* to own this album."

"I don't have a record player," Amy said as she

walked behind him to the next row of albums. "Does it come on CD?"

Tommy's mouth dropped open. "How could you not have a record player? This pains me."

"It's not like they're easy to find," Amy defended herself. "Where'd you get yours?"

"My grandma left hers to me after she died," Tommy said, replacing the record. "It's the only thing I ever got from anyone."

"That can't be true," Amy said, teasingly. "What about Christmas or your birthday?"

Tommy just looked at her and Amy's face fell. He had to be kidding. He'd *never* gotten a present?

"I don't want to bum you out with the details of my *E! True Hollywood Story*," he said, lowering his voice to a respectful—not ashamed—whisper. "But I don't mind hearing yours," he added, looking genuinely interested.

Amy's heart thumped. "I don't have any sad stories," she said, quickly moving on down the row and out the door.

"Riiiight," Tommy said, and followed her out into the cold.

A few short blocks later, Amy and Tommy were seated in a booth across from each other at Mama Joy's diner, the place everyone in Everwood seemed to end up at some point in their day. Amy sipped her hot tea, letting the pleasant warmth tingle through her. She felt as if every molecule in her body was sitting on the edge of its seat, wondering what was going to happen next.

"Sorry I was so out of it at the pharmacy the other day," Amy said. "It was just that guy shouting out the directions for my prescription . . ."

She almost shuddered at the memory of the pharmacist letting the world in on exactly how Amy should and shouldn't take her Zoloft.

"A lot of people are on antidepressants," Tommy said with a shrug. "It's not a big deal."

Amy's brain instantly conjured a picture of her father's disappointed and disapproving face. "It is to some people," she said.

"Yeah, well, those people don't understand depression," Tommy said. "I know what it's like to want to escape your body, your mind . . . your entire life."

Amy took this in and looked down into her tea. Everything felt so . . . heavy lately. Like she was being pressed down. She hated this feeling, but the fact that Tommy had even approached feeling the same way—it made her feel momentarily safe. She wished she could do the same for him, but their situations were totally different. At least she had gotten prescription, FDA-approved drugs. Tommy, apparently, had gone another route.

"I never really got into the whole drug scene, so—"

Tommy laughed, cutting her off, and shook his head.

"What? Why are you laughing?" Amy asked, confused.

"I'm guessing you heard the whole meth addict . . . rumor," he said.

Amy looked at him, feeling chagrined. As many times as she heard the adage "Don't believe everything you hear," she always seemed to do it anyway. It was exactly the kind of thing she would have scolded someone else for doing.

"So you never . . . ?"

"Meth?" Tommy said, shaking his head again. "No." Then he looked her in the eye, totally unabashed. "Pot? Yes."

Amy smirked and took a sip of her tea and Tommy smiled. It was great that he could joke about the things people said about him. Maybe one day she would be able to do the same with Page and Kayla's bathroom conversation, the very thought of which still made her blood curdle.

I'm not going to think about that now, Amy resolved. *I'm not going to let them ruin my night.*

And when Tommy suggested a walk, Amy couldn't get out of her seat fast enough.

"And I drank. I drank a lot," Tommy said.

Amy hugged herself against the cold. She and Tommy were talking and walking along the train tracks, something she hadn't done since the second grade when her parents had forbade her and Bright to go near them and Bright and Colin had dared Amy to do it anyway. Tommy kept surprising her—somehow reminding her that her world wasn't quite as small as she thought it was.

"And then . . . I wound up in rehab," he said. "Which, I mean . . . it sucked at first, but it helped. I'm clean now."

Amy smiled up at him, amazed at how straightforward and forthcoming he was, especially to a person he barely knew. It was nice being around someone who opened up so easily, especially when it meant all she was required to do was listen. If one more person asked her to share—to let it all out—she was going to scream. Of course, that would probably make people happy. They would probably love the amount of emotional outpouring a scream would indicate.

Tommy jumped down off the rail he was balancing on and walked over to the current, smallish train station. He plopped down on a bench and Amy followed, taking a seat next to him. They sat in silence for a few moments, watching their breath turn to steam, then disappear. Amy felt almost peaceful for the first time in months.

"So, you want to know what I heard about you?" Tommy asked out of nowhere.

Amy's stomach turned at the thought. "You didn't hear anything about me," she said. "You didn't even know my name until I told you, remember?"

"That's right," he said with a nod. "I forgot about that."

Amy smiled and leaned back into the bench. "But what were you going to say?" she asked. "I'm just curious."

"Well, I was gonna say that I heard you were the prettiest, most popular girl at County High, but you didn't care about that anymore," he said.

Amy's heart fell and she shifted uncomfortably. Was he just really good at this game, or was he messing with her?

"You checked your tiara at the door the day your boyfriend died, and you've been wandering the halls alone ever since, looking for something or someone to fill the void and take all the sadness away."

Okay, so he was messing with her. He did know who she was. Even as she was angry at him for pretending, she couldn't blame him for listening to what other people said about her. She had done the same to him, after all. But he had struck a chord. The peace inside her had been obliterated.

Amy wanted to suggest they go home. She wanted to get out of there and just sleep or cry or something, but she couldn't even make herself talk. She'd gone from okay to ridiculously sad in the space of two seconds. But somehow she felt grateful toward Tommy. He got it. He actually understood.

And then, it started to rain.

Tommy instantly sat up, but Amy didn't move. The rain seemed totally perfect at that moment.

"Here. Take this," Tommy said, shrugging out of his jacket. It wasn't until he put it around Amy's shoulders that she sat forward and snapped out of her trance a bit. Tommy put his arm around her and helped her up. She followed him past the train station and back out into the world.

By the time Tommy walked Amy back to her house, the rain had stopped and the sky was growing lighter. Amy had never spent the whole night out on the town and the idea that she had just gotten away with it was energizing. As she and Tommy started up the steps toward her front door, she barely even felt tired. Halfway up, Tommy paused and Amy continued to the landing.

"So," he said.

"So," Amy replied. "I should probably get inside."

"Probably," Tommy replied.

Amy didn't move, however. This felt like an end-of-date-kiss moment, except this wasn't really a date and she wasn't entirely sure she wanted to be kissed. But still, she didn't move. So maybe she did want to be kissed. Or at least she wanted to leave the option open.

"Yeah, it's probably really late," she said.

"Or really early," Tommy added, looking up at the sky.

"Oh . . . here," Amy said, suddenly remembering his jacket. She slipped out of its comforting warmth and returned it to him.

"Thanks," he said.

"Thank you," she replied. *For everything,* she added silently.

Tommy seemed to somehow read her thoughts, because just then he climbed the last couple of steps, leaned in, and kissed her. Amy barely had time to close her eyes, but she did have time to feel the softness of his lips and enjoy the flip-flop of her heart, something she hadn't been sure she was ever going to feel again.

When Tommy pulled back he was smiling, and Amy was too.

"I'll be seeing you," he said, backing up.

Amy watched him until he got to the sidewalk, trying to contain her silly grin. When she had left the house the night before, romance had been the last thing on her mind. Now, as she walked back in, it was a new day—and she had a whole new perspective.

CHAPTER 5

Ephram's life could not possibly have gotten any better. Not only had he found this amazing, beautiful girl, but she actually liked him back. That had never happened to him before—not once in his entire sixteen years. And just to make matters even better, she was at his house almost every day when he got home from school, ready and waiting to spend time with him. He didn't even have to ask to see her—she was *required* to be there. How perfect was that?

He slipped into his room on Wednesday afternoon and Madison followed, closing the door softly behind them. The mere sound of the click made his heart beat in anticipation. This was becoming a ritual—the post-school make-out session in his bedroom. They had stolen up here every day this week to sneak in some kissing time.

"You sure Delia's all right down there?" Ephram asked as Madison stepped closer to him.

"Please. I've gotten her so obsessed with *SportsCenter*, she's decided to become a sportscaster when she grows up," Madison said, biting her bottom lip in that adorable way of hers.

"Who knew you were an evil genius?" Ephram said as he slipped his arms around her. It was still amazing and unexpected, the fact that he could do this—the fact that she *wanted* him to do this.

"I have many layers," Madison said, looking up at him through her lashes.

"I can see that," he said.

Then he kissed her, sending his pulse into hyper drive. Together they stumbled toward the bed and fell onto it, sitting on the edge as Ephram pushed his hands into her hair and Madison grabbed one of the loopholes on his jeans to pull him closer to her. Ephram had to admit that doing this in his bedroom made it all the more exciting. He was getting away with a forbidden love affair right under his father's own roof. The irony was, it was the *only* place they could really fool around. Out in public people would point, talk, maybe even sneer. Plus there was the fact that technically his relationship with Madison was illegal.

It was so weird to think how much the outside world might care about this, when this was all there was. For Ephram, just then, Madison was his entire world. What could possibly be wrong with that?

"Hey! What're you guys—"

The bedroom door opened and Delia walked in. She stopped with her hand still on the doorknob and her jaw dropped. Ephram flew so far away from Madison he almost fell off the bed.

"What are you guys *doing*?" Delia asked.

Ephram looked at Madison, who paled so quickly he thought she might faint or barf, or both.

"Were you *kissing*?" Delia demanded.

Deny! Deny everything! Ephram's brain screamed.

"Yeah, sweetie, we were," Madison said.

Or you could take that tack, he thought. *Oh, God, now Dad's going to find out*. There was no way around it. He could practically see the wheels in his sister's brain turning. There was definite mileage to be gotten out of this situation. She would have to be an idiot not to see it, and Ephram knew his sister was no idiot.

"I don't think you're supposed to be doing that," she said, crossing her arms over her chest.

"Delia, you can't tell Dad," Ephram said, sitting forward.

"We're not supposed to keep secrets, Ephram," she said, looking at him as if she were the elder and he the much younger sibling.

Ephram wasn't proud of it, but his mind started flipping through all the little things Delia had done recently that he had kept secret out of brotherly love. Like when she'd left her bike outside overnight in the rain. Or when she'd dropped that black marker on the living room rug and they'd moved the big chair over a few inches to cover the stain. None of it was enough for blackmail against *this*.

"Okay," Ephram said finally, hanging his head. "What do you want?"

Delia smiled, excited. "You guys have to take me miniature golfing once a week. Both of you."

"Deal," Madison said, starting to get up.

"That's not all," Delia said seriously.

Madison glanced at Ephram, half impressed, half scared, and sat down again.

"I also want to go to Sal's for dinner tonight and I want an entire roll of quarters for the video games," she said.

"No problem," Ephram told her. "But that's it."

"Fine, but don't do this again when I'm in the house," Delia said, rolling her eyes as she turned away. "It's icky."

She walked off, closing the door behind her. Ephram took one look at Madison and they both burst out laughing—a combination of relief and total amusement.

"Your sister drives a hard bargain," Madison said finally, reaching out for Ephram's hand.

"She's a Brown," Ephram said. "We don't stop till we get what we want."

Madison smiled and planted a long, slow kiss on his lips. "Tell me about it."

The Everwood Library was hushed and still, save for the sound of the dimes dropping into the copy machine in the back corner and the whir of the little engine as it photocopied. Somewhere off in the children's reading room a little girl laughed. Amy followed Tommy down an aisle marked *Photography* and ran her fingers along the plastic-covered spines of the books. She hadn't set foot in this place since last year's Civil War research paper. She had forgotten how much she loved the mingling scents of crisp new books and musty old volumes. When was the last time she had even picked up a book for fun?

"Ahh . . . here's what I'm looking for," Tommy said, sliding a huge but thin book out from the bottom shelf.

Amy checked the spine. "Jacques-Henri Lartique?"

"He's this amazing photographer," Tommy said, sitting down on the carpeted floor. He placed his stack of books to be borrowed next to him—books by William S. Burroughs, Jack Kerouac, Hunter S. Thompson.

For a person who had missed enough school to be held back a year, Tommy was definitely a big reader. When he had suggested a date at the library, Amy had thought he was kidding, but it turned out every woman that worked in this place knew Tommy by name and face. He was quite popular among the old biddies.

And to think I almost wrote him off before I even got to know him, Amy thought, gathering up her long scarf in her lap as she sat next to him. Tommy was smarter and more well-read than any guy who went to County.

"Check it out," Tommy said, opening to the center of the book. It was a black-and-white photograph of an old-fashioned race car that was zooming out the right side of the frame. It was shot at an angle and the spectators on the sidewalk were blurred and stretched.

"Wow. That's so cool," Amy said, feeling as if she should try to find something more insightful to say.

"There's so much movement in his photographs," Tommy said, flipping to another page, which featured a biplane trying to take off. "It's like they're not actually still, you know?"

"Like he was really trying to capture life in motion," Amy said, pulling the book toward her lap.

"Exactly," Tommy said, his face lighting up. "I knew you'd get it."

Amy smiled, pleased at the compliment, and turned the page. The next photograph made her pause. It depicted a woman with her face turned away from the camera, looking down and out of the frame. Her brown hair was swept back from her face and her arms were crossed over her chest, holding herself. She wore nothing but a plain robe.

"It's so lonely," Amy said, clutching the book with both hands.

"Depressing, huh?" Tommy asked, reaching over to flip the page.

"Actually I really like it," Amy said. "It makes me feel . . . I don't know . . . something."

Tommy smiled. "Well, good. That's what good art is supposed to do, right?"

"Yeah, I guess," Amy said. She couldn't take her eyes off the page. "I wonder if you can buy prints of his work."

Tommy glanced around and slid the book out of Amy's hands. He grasped the top of the page in his fingertips and suddenly Amy realized what he was about to do.

"Tommy!" she whispered, her heart thumping with fear.

"What? You love it. You should have it," Tommy said.

"You can't rip apart a library book," she said, tucking her chin.

"Look, these books are public property," Tommy said with a shrug. "They're as much yours as they are anyone else's and you obviously really love the picture. Why shouldn't you have it?"

Amy smiled slightly, touched, but she was also

horrified at the idea that he was perfectly willing to sit right there and destroy public property in her name. She reached over and slipped it back out of his hands, replacing it on the shelf.

"You're sweet, but no," she said.

"Okay," Tommy said, standing and grabbing his books. "I'm gonna go check these out. Meet you by the door?"

"Sure," Amy said with a nod. She stood in the aisle until he was gone and then took a deep breath, feeling almost relieved to be alone. Clearly Tommy had a skewed vision of right and wrong.

Still, it was kind of cool that he was willing to break the law for her. Not the bring-this-guy-home-to-daddy kind of cool, but still pretty cool. Amy smiled and slipped out of the aisle. Maybe her dad would never meet Tommy, but what was wrong with that? It might be kind of fun to have her own life—to be the girl with the secret for once.

On the Tuesday before Thanksgiving, Ephram pulled up in front of his house right behind Madison, who was just parking her car. Ephram hadn't exactly *planned* to get home at the exact same time he knew Madison was showing up to help out with dinner, but was it his fault if piano practice had ended half an hour early due to severe stomach cramps?

Okay, so maybe he *had* planned it.

He got out of his car and slammed the door, already smiling giddily. Madison whirled around, took one look at him, and smiled back. Ephram still hadn't gotten used to the heady feeling he experienced every time he was reminded that Madison actually liked him. It was beyond amazing.

"Hey," he said, walking up to her.

"Hey," she replied.

"My dad won't be home for, like, fifteen minutes," Ephram said. "Want to take advantage of me?"

Madison laughed and shook her head. "We promised Delia . . . ."

"Delia's not here," he said, tugging on her hand and leading her toward the front door. "She's over at Nina's until we decide otherwise."

"Ephram . . ." Madison protested lamely. Definitely not a real protest. He whipped out his keys and opened the front door.

"Hello?" he called out, sticking his head inside.

Total silence.

"Hello?" He stepped in and let Madison through as well. "See? Nobody's home," Ephram said. "I told you."

He leaned forward to try to kiss her, but Madison pushed his shoulder and turned away playfully.

"I have to get Delia, and your dad could be home any minute," she told him.

Ephram grabbed both her hands, leaned up against the doorjamb between the living room and the kitchen, and pulled her to him.

"Your nose is all red," he told her.

"Ephram, we can't," Madison said, struggling, but not too much. "We made a pact."

"I can't be tied to some pact when you're standing here with your nose all cute and red," Ephram told her, slipping his hands to her waist. "I'm sorry. I just can't."

Madison smiled and let him kiss her. It was quick, but he was making progress.

"We said we wouldn't do anything in the house," Madison told him. "What if he comes in?"

"I'll lock the door," Ephram said.

"Like he wouldn't figure that out," Madison replied. "The man's a brain surgeon, Ephram."

She took one step away from him and already Ephram missed having her in his arms.

"Don't let the fancy title fool you. My dad's totally clueless," he said, following her into the living room. "We could be making out on top of him and he would have no idea."

He grabbed her hand again and she turned to kiss him, a little less quickly this time. Still, she wasn't quite ready to give up the lecture.

"You know, if we don't tell him, he's just going to find out on his own," she said.

"He won't find out. He's in his own world half

the time," Ephram said. "I spilled Coke all over the couch the other night, right? He told me to clean it up, but as soon as he left the room, I just flipped the pillow over. The man is dense."

"No, he's not," Madison said. "And you should be thankful you have such a cool dad."

Ephram rolled his eyes. "He's cool when you're here," he said. "Come by in the morning, I swear you'll be astounded by his lameness. I promise."

He leaned in to kiss her again, but this time she pulled away.

"Ephram, we can't. It's wrong."

"Okay, how about this?" Ephram said. "I'll tell my dad about us when you show me how to do that tongue curl thing you were talking about."

Madison grinned and Ephram knew he had her. He kissed her on the mouth and held her tight.

"Five minutes," she said. "But then we get Delia."

Acting on a whim, Ephram pushed her backward onto the couch and fell on top of her. Madison screeched and laughed in surprise, wrapping her arms around his neck. Ephram was just trailing a bunch of kisses down her cheekbone when suddenly there was a huge crash. They both sat up, hearts in their throats, to find Ephram's father bursting out of the closet.

The closet?! Ephram thought.

"Dad!" he said, shocked.

"Dr. Brown!" Madison put in, struggling to sit up with Ephram on top of her.

"What the hell is going on?!" Ephram's father shouted.

Suddenly Ephram was sitting on one side of the couch, Madison on the other, while his father ranted and paced in front of them. Ephram's mind reeled, trying to think back to everything that had just been said while his father was apparently watching them through the slats in the closet door.

Oh God! *We talked about making out. We talked about tongue curls,* Ephram thought, his stomach turning. *But most of all I talked about how very lame my father is. . . .*

"This is beyond unacceptable!" his father was shouting. "This is in some other universe of unacceptability!"

"Dad, I think you're overreacting a little," Ephram began, trying to sound reasonable.

"Overreacting? I think not!" his dad shouted. "Maybe you think this is just another example of my uncool lameness, Ephram, but I don't think it would be possible to overreact to this. How long has this been going on?"

"Not long," Madison piped up. "I wanted to tell you—"

"So I heard. Right after the tongue curling lessons," Ephram's dad said sarcastically. "It's a good thing I was in that closet just now."

Ephram sensed a small opening—an opportunity for righteous indignation that might throw some of the attention off his own indiscretions. Maybe.

"Yeah, what's that about, anyway?" he asked. "You're spying on me now? Whatever happened to the right to privacy?"

"When you're sixteen there *is* no privacy. *This* is why there is no privacy when you're sixteen," he added, pointing at them. *"This!"*

Indignation rebuffed, Ephram glanced at Madison. There had to be some way out of this mess. There just had to be.

"Look, this whole thing was sort of an accident from the beginning," Madison told his father. "It started out as more of a kissing thing, and then it just kinda—"

Watching Madison try to explain away what they had was torture. Ephram had to interrupt.

"This is none of your business," he told his father, his eyes flashing.

"'None of my business'?" his father replied. "She's twenty, you're sixteen. I hired her. I brought her into this house. I think aiding and abetting a felony makes it my business."

"So I'm sixteen. So what?" Ephram snapped. "Would it be better if I was having sex with someone my own age?

"Ephram!" Madison gasped. "We didn't have

sex, Dr. Brown," she said. "I swear. No sex at all."

Ephram's father looked as if he was about to be sick, but he held it together—barely.

"The fact is, Madison isn't your age and whether you like it or not, that makes all the difference," he said. "My first thought is to fire you," he said, looking at Madison. "Then to kill you," he told Ephram. "And then to kill you a little, too," he added, returning to Madison. He took a deep breath and shook his head at the floor. "Here's what we're going to do. Firing you would be unfair to Delia, who is the only one I don't want to suffer for this. Whatever has been going on between you two is over. Now."

"No way!" Ephram exclaimed, panicking.

"Completely and permanently," his father said, throwing out his hands, palms down. "We're going to travel back in time before any of this ever happened and we're going to start over. Understood?"

"This is such bull—"

"Totally," Madison interjected, causing Ephram's lungs to constrict. Was she kidding? "This whole thing was a mistake. It never should have happened. I'm sorry, Dr. Brown."

Ephram couldn't believe the betrayal. He stared at her, feeling like he'd offered her up his heart on a silver platter and she'd just taken a steak knife to it. No matter how hard he glared, she wouldn't even look at him. Ephram hadn't felt so alone in a long time.

"Madison, you should leave now," his dad said, causing her to bolt instantly up. "Ephram, go to your room."

He barely heard the second demand. "Madison," Ephram said, rising as she fled for the door.

"Don't even think about it," his father said in a very no-nonsense tone. "You do, she's fired. And you're grounded for life."

Ephram was trapped. He felt as if he'd just opened the most expensive, most perfect gift—something he'd been longing and hoping for, looking at in store windows his entire life—and then had it snatched right out of his grasp by his own father. Why was he doing this to Ephram? How *could* he do it?

Unfortunately he knew there was nothing he could say or do in that moment that would get through to his father, not when his dad was in this high-and-mighty maniacal state. So he just glared at his father, all the happiness he'd felt only minutes ago ripped to shreds at his feet, then stomped upstairs. But even the slam of his door could do nothing to numb the anger and pain. His perfect, ridiculously giddy relationship with Madison could not be over. There was no way Ephram was going to let this happen.

As soon as she was freed from school for the four-day weekend, Amy went directly to the pharmacy.

She walked in and caught Tommy's eye. He was behind the counter ringing up a huge order for a middle-aged man, and he smiled when he saw her. Amy ducked down an aisle to wait for him, knowing that he'd come up with an excuse to come see her. It was nice that Tommy worked in one of the most frequented businesses in Everwood. It meant that she could be with him any time she wanted. Easy-access dating.

"Hey."

Amy glanced up from the stationery display and saw Tommy at the end of the aisle.

"Hey," she said.

"Wanna walk outside?" he asked.

"Well, I'm really here to check out the new shipment of Post-its," Amy joked.

Tommy grabbed her hand in his and gently pulled her toward the door. Out on the sidewalk they swung their hands between them until they got to the alley next to the store. Then Tommy leaned in to give her a quick kiss.

"My shift's over in ten minutes if you want to hang out the rest of the day," he said.

"I would love to, but my grandparents flew in from Arizona today," Amy said. "I was supposed to be home half an hour ago."

"Well, that should be fun, right?" Tommy said, putting his hands in his pockets. "Big family turkey thing."

"Oh, it's a party," Amy said sarcastically. "Three generations of people who hate each other fighting over who gets the white meat."

Tommy laughed.

"I guess it's probably the same at your house, right?" she asked.

"We don't really do holidays at my house," Tommy said. "Not so big on traditions."

"You're kidding," she said. "So what're you going to do tomorrow night?"

"I don't know. Probably nothing."

Amy's face fell slightly. First the comment about never getting any gifts and now no holidays? It seemed so sad. Tommy didn't deserve to be alone on Thanksgiving.

"You have to come to my house," she said decidedly. Then, seeing he was about to protest, she added, "There's gonna be like a thousand people there anyway. It's not like one more is gonna kill anyone. And my mom makes this awesome cranberry thing that I think you would love."

Tommy reached out and gently pushed Amy's bangs back from her face. "You're really sweet, aren't you?"

Amy flushed. "No. I just—"

Tommy was leaning in to kiss her again, when the last voice Amy had expected to hear stopped them cold.

"I don't believe we've met," her grandmother said.

Amy yanked her hand away from Tommy's and turned around. Sure enough, Grandma Harper was standing right behind her, leather jacket, motorcycle goggles, and all.

"Grandma . . ."

"Edna Harper," she said, extending her hand to Tommy. "Amy's favorite grandmother."

"Hi. Tommy Callahan," he said, shaking hands with her. He smiled at Amy like he thought her grandma was amusing. Amy wanted to die.

"Well, I've gotta get back to work, but it was a pleasure to meet you, Mrs. Harper," he said. "I guess I'll see you tomorrow at dinner."

Amy smiled, happy that he was saying he would come. Her grandmother shot her a look and Amy stared back. *Don't say anything embarrassing,* she willed silently.

"I guess you will," her grandma said without missing a beat.

Tommy nodded at Amy and disappeared around the corner. Amy looked down at the ground, prepping herself for the upcoming round of twenty questions.

"Who's the new copilot?" her grandmother asked.

"Nobody," Amy said, lifting her head and shrugging. "Just a guy."

"Just a guy my boots," she replied. "No granddaughter of mine goes around holding hands with a guy who's 'just a guy.'"

Amy smiled and looked away. Maybe Tommy was more than just a guy, but she wished she would have been able to figure that out before the family interference began. Of course, she probably should have thought of that before her knee-jerk invitation to Thanksgiving dinner. Damn.

"See you and your friend at the big Turkey Day gorge-athon," Edna said, and then she mercifully walked off.

Amy leaned back against the wall and sighed. She should have known Grandma wasn't going to torture her. Unfortunately her parents were nothing like Edna Harper. But who knew? Maybe they would surprise her tomorrow.

A person could dream . . . right?

That very afternoon, Ephram was in his room when he heard Madison's car pull up outside. He went to the window and watched the headlights extinguish, watched her get out and tentatively approach the house. His heart went out to her— she must have been so uncomfortable, thanks to his insane father. But he was also proud of her. Not many people would have had the guts to come back to this nuthouse. It buoyed his confidence that she refused to be scared away.

All he wanted to do was run downstairs and talk to her, but his dad was down there—a lurking presence waiting to keep a hawk's eye on their every move. So instead he sat down at his desk and stared at a page in his history book until he heard the back door close and his father's truck pull out of the drive. He was off to Mama Joy's to pick up dinner. That gave Ephram fifteen to twenty whole minutes.

Heart racing, he jogged downstairs and into the kitchen where Delia and Madison were hard at work making Thanksgiving decorations, surrounded by arts and crafts supplies. Madison looked up when she heard him coming, but barely grazed him with her eyes before looking down again. Ephram tried not to let it affect him. She was upset. Of course she was.

"Hey. Looks like you're running low on construction paper," he told Delia.

"It's okay. I have more in my room," she told him.

"If you go get it, I'll help you guys out," he replied.

Delia's little face lit up at the suggestion and she bolted by him for the stairs. For about two seconds, Ephram felt guilty for leading her on, but he had no other ideas on how to get Madison alone. And he needed to get her alone.

"Madison—"

"Please don't," she said, her hand trembling slightly as she shoved markers back into their box.

"Don't what?" he asked, swallowing hard. "I'm

just trying to figure out what's going on here."

"Nothing is going on," she replied firmly. "It can't. You heard your dad—"

"Screw my dad," Ephram said. "I don't care what he says."

"Well, *I* care what he says," she replied, slapping the box down on the kitchen island and finally really looking at him. "And he's not totally wrong, either."

Yes. Yes he is.

"How could he not be wrong when he doesn't even know what we're about?" Ephram demanded.

"We're not about anything. *We* are not anything," she said, tearing his heart out. "Not anymore."

"Why? 'Cause he said so?" Ephram asked, holding on by a thread. "You can't just turn your feelings off like that."

"Yeah. I can," she said flatly.

Ephram took a breath, letting the searing pain of that one pass before he spoke again. "I don't believe you."

"Look, I knew what we were doing was wrong, I knew it wouldn't work, and I knew it would be worse if we didn't tell your dad," Madison rambled. "I'm three for three and I'm gonna quit now."

"You said you liked me," Ephram said. "You said I made you undone. I'm not exactly sure what that means, but I know it's a good thing and I know it doesn't just go away—not when you really care for somebody. There's no way you don't still have those feelings."

What am I saying? Have a little dignity, man! But Ephram didn't care. His heart was already on the line. He had to do everything he could to save it.

"Ephram, I can't," Madison said, sounding like she wanted out of this conversation. But Ephram wasn't letting her off that easy.

"That's not the same thing," he said. "'Can't' is because of my dad. 'Don't' is because of you."

Madison looked at the counter. They were both breathing heavily as if they had been through a grueling workout. Ephram almost did feel as if he had just run a mile. This was taking that much out of him.

Suddenly Delia jumped to the bottom of the stairs and ran into the room carrying a stack of paper.

"I brought the green down too," she announced happily, unaware of what she had just walked in on. "Just in case."

Ephram ignored her. At the moment there was only Madison.

"'Can't' or 'don't,'" he said. "Just tell me."

She looked up into his eyes and said it. One word. Without even blinking.

"Don't."

And that one word pretty much killed him.

CHAPTER 6

Thanksgiving Day arrived—a day that was supposed to be fun and lighthearted, even exciting and romantic, considering Madison was supposed to be spending it with Ephram and his family. But instead of flirting by the fire while the turkey roasted away, Ephram found himself in front of the sink, taking out his aggression on a stack of innocent potatoes while Madison chopped up beans for a salad behind him. His father stood at the end of the center island working on some carrots, making stupid remarks every few seconds in an attempt to pretend everything was normal.

Just to rub salt in the open wound, Delia was taping the whole thing with the video camera.

"How are those potatoes coming?" Ephram's father asked in his chipper voice, mugging for the camera so that twenty years from now they could all see how he was trying to break the tension. He couldn't possibly think they wouldn't all remember what had really been going on, right? "No fingertips in there yet, I hope."

You suck, Ephram thought with each swipe of the peeler. *You suck, you suck, you suck.*

"Ephram, you have to stand closer to Madison to be in the little box," Delia told him, watching through the LCD screen.

"Enough with the camera, Delia," he said over his shoulder.

"It's the new tradition, remember?" she said. "You started it last year."

Yeah. What was I thinking? Ephram wondered.

"Okay, Madison," Delia said. "You have to look in the camera and tell me what you're thankful for."

Ephram glanced over again and saw his father pause in his chopping. Madison glanced at his dad, then looked down again, quickly wiping her hands on her apron. She was visibly upset and all Ephram wanted to do was hug her. He should be *allowed* to hug the girl he cared about. Especially when she was sad. Especially on a national freakin' holiday.

"Okay . . . um . . . this just needs to marinate for a couple of hours," Madison said shakily. "And as far as the turkey goes—"

"You're not leaving, are you?" Delia asked.

"I have to, sweetie."

There were tears in her voice. Audible, horrifying tears.

"But you said your family went to Florida for Thanksgiving and you'd eat here with us," Delia said.

Madison turned away quickly and knocked a hot pan on the stove with her hand.

"Ouch! Dammit!" she said, bringing the wound to her mouth.

Ephram instantly grabbed a towel and ran it under some cold water.

"Let me look at that," his father said, coming over.

But Ephram got between him and Madison. "I got it," he said.

"I'm fine, really," Madison protested.

Ephram pressed the cool towel into her hand and Madison looked into his eyes. He knew it. He knew she was lying when she said her feelings for him were history. They so weren't. He could feel it more palpably that she could feel the stupid burn. And she knew he could see it. Her eyes teared up right in front of him, and not from the pain in her hand.

"I'm sorry, I . . . I have to go," she said, quickly sidestepping Ephram. She was about to burst into tears. They could all tell.

"But you're coming back, right?" Delia asked, sounding desperate.

"I don't think so," Madison said.

"Tomorrow, though?" Delia pressed, refusing to give up. "You'll be back tomorrow."

Madison tried to smile for Delia. "I can't come back anymore, honey," she said, glancing over her shoulder at Ephram as she moved toward the door. "I'm sorry. I just can't."

She grabbed her jacket and walked out, leaving Delia in stunned silence. Ephram would have given anything to follow her, but an even bigger part of him wanted to give it to his father.

"You did this," he said, his tone full of venom as he glared at his dad.

"Honey, could you go up to your room for a minute, please?" his father said to Delia.

"No," she replied.

"You couldn't stand that I was finally happy," Ephram shouted. "You hated that I had somebody and you didn't."

"It was wrong, Ephram. And I couldn't just let it go," he said. "Madison knew that and she agreed with me."

"She agreed because you threatened her," Ephram told him.

"Why did you threaten Madison?" Delia said. "Don't you like her?"

"Of course I like her," his father replied. "But not for dating your brother."

Delia snapped her mouth closed at that point,

probably worried that Ephram thought she had told on him.

"You say you want me to grow up, but you don't," Ephram told him. "You just want me to stay a kid so you can do all your stupid father-son stuff that you missed out on and feel guilty about. Well, it's too late. I'm a man and I'm going to make my own decisions."

Ephram stalked out of the kitchen, heading for the stairs. He had had just about enough familial bonding for one Turkey Day, thank you very much.

"You're not a man," his father said, coming after him. "If you were you'd realize how childish you're being right now. Upsetting your sister, blaming me for your mistakes. I am sorry you're hurting and I'm sure this is very difficult for Madison as well, but the two of you put me in an impossible situation."

Ephram stopped halfway up the stairs and came back down to the landing. Why was everything always about his father?

"How can something be impossible if it's happening?" he demanded, looking down hatefully at his dad. "It was. It was great and you couldn't deal, so you *made* it impossible. You make my entire life impossible."

"This isn't a question of what I can deal with, Ephram."

"Yes, it is!" Ephram exploded. "You're alone.

That's your problem, okay? That's fine. I'm not you. I don't want to be like you. If Madison and I want this that's all that matters."

"That's not all that matters," his dad said.

"I shouldn't have to be alone just because you are," Ephram shot back.

Then, as he seemed to be doing more and more often lately, he retreated quickly to his room.

"I think it's so cool that you got my mom flowers," Amy said, taking Tommy's hand as they walked up the front steps to her house on Thanksgiving Day. It was beautiful and sunny and Amy was actually feeling good about bringing Tommy home. Her mother had seemed psyched when she said she was bringing a friend and even her dad couldn't find fault with a guy who came bearing gifts.

"I hope she likes them," Tommy said as Amy opened the door.

She had a feeling he was more concerned with her mom liking *him,* so she squeezed his hand and smiled up at him. "She will."

As soon as they were inside Amy could smell the delicious scents of Thanksgiving—the gravy, turkey, stuffing, and mashed potatoes. Everyone was already seated at the table as she and Tommy walked in, coming up behind her father who was about to start carving.

"Everybody, this is Tommy," Amy said with a

smile. "Tommy, this is my mom and . . . everybody."

Amy's aunt Linda, her grandmother and Irv, and Grandma and Grandpa Roberts all said hello. Amy's dad simply shot her a scathing look, which Amy chose to ignore. She wasn't sure what she had done this time, but it was Thanksgiving. She wasn't going to let him get to her.

"Hi," Tommy said, holding the flowers out to Amy's mom. "Thank you for having me, Mrs. Abbott."

Amy's mother beamed at him, impressed. "Thank you," she said.

Amy glanced at her aunt Linda who smiled encouragingly. Tommy already had them in the palm of his hand.

"You're late," her father said sternly.

Well, all of them but Dad, Amy thought, pulling out a chair.

"That's my fault, sir," Tommy said. "The only flowers left at the first place were kinda dead, so I drove around looking for another place that was open. I'm really sorry."

"Well, isn't he sweet as apple pie," Grandma Roberts said. "I want him to sit here," she added, patting the chair next to hers.

Tommy and Amy both sat and Amy placed her napkin in her lap. She could feel the tension coming off her father in waves and wondered what his problem was. So she was late. Big deal. Tommy had explained and it wasn't like they had started eating yet.

"You going to carve that thing, Harold? Or should we just tear into it with our hands?" Grandma Roberts asked.

Amy smiled privately. If she couldn't stick it to her dad, at least her mom's mom never missed a chance.

For a few minutes the table was occupied with *please pass the's* and *can I have a little more's*. Amy and Tommy stole little glances at each other as they dished up their food. It was nice having Tommy among her family. It felt right. Or as right as anything could feel these days.

"Hmmmm. Who made the plum gravy?" Grandma Roberts asked, sounding pleased.

"Dad makes it very year," Bright said, shoveling food into his mouth. "Good, huh?"

"There's more hairs than plums in it," she replied, changing her tune completely.

"Mother . . . ," Amy's mom scolded.

Amy bit back a wry laugh. Her family was just too predictable sometimes. She looked at her father to gauge his reaction, but he was just staring straight at Tommy as he chewed. It was like he hadn't even heard the insult.

"So, how long have you known my daughter?" he asked with no preface.

Amy's heart skipped a beat. *Here we go. . . .*

"Uh, I don't know," Tommy said, wiping his mouth with his napkin. "I guess about two weeks now," he said, glancing at her for confirmation. Amy nodded slightly and prayed that was all her dad had up his sleeve. Unfortunately, she knew better.

"And how old are you?"

"I am seventeen," Tommy said.

"Dad, can we just eat, please?" Amy asked, already feeling for Tommy.

"I'm just trying to get to know the boy," her father said with that superior tone in his voice. "You're seventeen, huh? But I understand you're still a junior. Normally you'd be a year ahead of Amy, right?"

"Harold!" Amy's mom said.

"That's okay, Mrs. Abbott," Tommy said patiently. "I took some time off."

He took some time off, okay? Satisfied? Amy thought, staring at her father. *Leave him alone.*

"I notice you're not with your family tonight. Did they kick you out for some reason?" her father said.

Omigod, omigod, omigod, Amy thought. This was a perfect nightmare. She couldn't believe she had invited Tommy over here to be badgered.

"Um, no," he said, shifting in his seat. "We don't really do holidays at my house."

"That's a pity. Although I supposed a family doesn't have much cause to rejoice when their son is a known felon."

"Dad!" Amy blurted out, her heart shriveling to the size of a pea. She was mortified. Completely and totally mortified—for Tommy, for herself, and even for her father who was making himself look like a total bastard.

"Harold, come on now," Irv said.

"I think I should go," Tommy said, pushing his chair back.

This was not happening. This could not be happening.

"Oh, piddle paddle," Grandma Roberts said. "Just ignore the man. That's what the rest of us do."

"That's okay. Thank you for dinner, Mrs. Abbott," Tommy said, stepping away. "Nice meeting you all."

Amy got up and followed Tommy to the door. She didn't even know where to begin.

"Tommy, I'm so sorry," she said as he grabbed his jacket. "He's such a jerk."

"No, it's okay," Tommy said. "I'm used to people believing all the rumors about me."

"But I . . . I invited you here and he—"

Oh, God, how she wanted to kill her father just then.

"Really. It's fine," Tommy said, straightening his jacket. "I don't want to cause any trouble. I'll just call you later." He gave her a quick kiss and was out the door before she could even put together another sentence.

Amy couldn't believe how amazing Tommy was being about this. Her father had cruelly insulted him in front of a table full of people and he wasn't even mad. How could her father do this to her? He'd just driven away the one person who possibly gave a crap about her in the entire world and he'd done it without a single shred of regret.

As soon as she heard Tommy's car pull away, Amy turned and headed for the stairs. There was no way she could go back to that table. No way in hell.

"Where do you think you're going?" her father shouted, coming out into the living room.

"To my room," Amy said. She was so furious she was shaking.

"That boy is not allowed back in this house ever again. Is that clear?" her father yelled.

"Fine!" Amy shouted, angry tears springing to her eyes. "I'll just go to his place from now on."

"No, you will not," he said.

Amy walked into the center of the room. Over her father's shoulder she could see her entire family sitting at the table, hands in their laps, a huge gray cloud hovering over them.

"What are you gonna do about it?" Amy asked.

"Who do you think you're talking to?" he

demanded, narrowing his eyes. "I drove to Wyoming to pick you up during one of your cries for help. I put you on the antidepressants that you begged me for. But I will not have my daughter dating some crystal meth junkie—"

Amy was so frustrated she could have burst right out of her skin. "Oh my God! He's not—"

"You try to see him again, I'll put a bolt on your bedroom door," her father said, not even bothering to try to listen to her. "You don't believe it? Watch me."

"Dad—" Amy could barely get a word out past the sob choking her throat.

"And the fact that you kept this boy a secret only proves how manipulative you've become," her father said. "Springing him on us during Thanksgiving when we have guests? No . . . no. Your behavior is no longer a by-product of some mysterious depression. It's malicious and intentional and it is over. From now on you will have no car, no TV, no phone, no Internet. I will take you to school and I will pick you up and you will not leave this house otherwise. This self-indulgent act of yours is going to stop right now."

Amy couldn't believe her father was speaking to her this way. All she had done was brought home a friend—pretty much the only friend she had left in the world right now—and he was punishing her for it. Didn't he know how miserable her life was?

Couldn't he see how much *more* miserable he was making it?

"You think that by keeping me prisoner in my own house you're going to save me?" she said, barely holding back the tears. "From what? Tommy? You don't even know him. As far as I can see, the only person I need to be saved from anymore is you."

"Amy!" her mother said.

"I hate this house. I hate my school. I hate my friends. And I hate this family," Amy said. "I hate everything about my entire, stupid life. So you can ground me, Dad. You can yell at me. Do whatever you want. Because honestly? I wish I was dead. I don't feel anything anymore. And you know the best part? I don't even care."

With that, Amy stormed out and ran up to her room, slamming the door behind her. She put her hand over her mouth and cried, holding her waist tightly with her other arm. That outburst should have felt good. It should have felt like she was getting everything off her chest. But she only felt more trapped than ever, with all those people downstairs judging her, thinking she was some kind of spoiled delinquent. No one cared how she really felt. No one wanted her to be happy. They just wanted her to go back to being the old Amy so they could pretend nothing was wrong. But she couldn't do it. She couldn't be that person anymore. She wasn't even sure of who that person was.

Colin had died. And he'd taken the old Amy with him.

I have to get out of here, Amy thought as the muffled voices of her family started up again. *I can't stay here. I can't.*

She yanked her backpack out of her closet and threw it on the bed. Opening drawers at random, she shoved underwear, socks, a couple of pairs of jeans, and some sweaters into the bag. Then she turned around in her room wildly, making sure there was nothing else she needed. Her eyes fell on the framed picture of her and Colin by her bed and she grabbed it and threw that in the bag as well. She locked her bedroom door, shouldered the bag, and crawled out the window onto the low roof over the front porch. Sliding her feet as she walked to the edge, she just hoped she wouldn't fall. The last thing she needed was to be treated by her father for a broken leg. Then she would really be trapped.

At the edge of the roof, Amy tossed her bag onto the grass, slid down, and pushed herself over until she was hanging from the lowest point. Closing her eyes and saying a quick prayer, she dropped down to the ground and crouched. No problem.

She stood up and took a deep breath. She was free. Now all she had to do was figure out where the hell she was going.

• • •

That night, after a lonely, pointless, anger-filled Thanksgiving dinner, Ephram's father went out and Ephram decided enough was enough. He had to see Madison, had to make sure she was okay. And he needed to know where she stood. Because if he was going to really stand up to his father on this one, he needed her by his side.

After convincing Delia that they needed to win Madison back for both their sakes, the two of them drove together over to the little house Madison shared with another college student on the outskirts of town. He stopped the car in front of her house, paused, and took a deep breath. This was it—the moment of truth. Whatever Madison said now was going to decide whether or not he was going to be miserable for the rest of his life.

"Are you going in there or what?" Delia asked.

"Yeah," Ephram said. He couldn't wimp out in front of a ten-year-old. "Yeah, I'm going right now."

He got out of the car and tried to ignore his quaking knees as he approached the door. Madison responded to the bell so quickly it was like she was waiting for him. But the look on her face said otherwise. She opened the storm door, but didn't step out or invite him in.

"Ephram, please . . . ," she said, shaking her head.

"You were right. We should've told my dad right away," he said.

"I don't think it would have made a difference."

"Maybe, maybe not," he said. "But it would have been the more adult way to handle it. And from now on, I'm going to be more adult when it comes to me and you."

"Ephram—"

"Look, you may have had a million boyfriends already, but I've never had a real girlfriend," Ephram said, laying it all out there. "I've never actually liked a girl who liked me back in the same way, at the same time. I think it's something I have to fight for."

There. That sounded manly enough.

"Fight how?" she said. "Your dad is not gonna change his mind."

"Screw my dad," Ephram replied. "He can't stop this. At the end of the day, the only person who can is you."

Madison looked at him for a moment and he could practically see her insides melting. Whatever he had just said, it had been the right thing. She took a deep breath and let it out slowly.

"So let's say we can convince him," she said. "What about everyone else? Your friends, my friends . . . the government?"

"Bush has his hands full," Ephram joked. "And as far as my friends go, I've only got two. And you're one of them, so . . . how would you feel about me dating Madison?"

Madison laughed slightly and looked at the ground. When her eyes met his again, she was smiling for real.

"I dunno," she said. "She is a pretty cool chick."

Yes! Ephram thought. He stepped up onto the door stop and kissed her. She closed her eyes and kissed him right back. It was over. He'd won. Madison was all his.

When she pulled away she glanced over his shoulder and made a clicking sound with her tongue. "Go get your sister," she said. "She must be an icicle by now."

Ephram turned to see Delia's hopeful face in the window of the car and smiled. Everything was going to be all right. He was going to make sure of it.

A few hours after crawling out her bedroom window, Amy found herself wandering the streets of Denver alone. As soon as she left her house and started walking for the bus station (she knew if she started her car in the driveway her parents would hear), she had called Tommy. But his cell phone went straight to voicemail no matter how many times she tried. The longer she walked, the more her thoughts turned to Colin and how much he had loved Thanksgiving. He used to steal the wishbone from his house every year and run over so he could break it with Bright. Until his last

Thanksgiving, of course. That year he'd shared it with Amy.

Thinking about Colin had helped her choose a destination. Denver was the last place she had seen him, when they had said good-bye for the last time. Denver was where she needed to be.

Once she was there, she felt peaceful. No one in this city knew who she was, or cared what she had done. Amy wandered the streets of the city, stopping to rest now and again on a bench or a doorstep. Groups of people bustled by her on the street, rushing to dinner or from one party to the next. Most businesses were closed because of the holiday, but some of the restaurants were lit up and full of noise, open for people who would rather not spend their Thanksgiving slaving over the stove. Amy stopped in front of one such establishment, looking in at the warm, smiling faces. Everyone was together and happy, having a good time.

For the first time, Amy felt the slightest pang of regret for leaving her family. She walked for hours, picturing them around the table, talking, eating, telling stories . . . and suddenly she had never felt so alone.

What was she doing here? She had no money, no place to stay. And sure, walking around by herself for the past few hours had been sort of freeing, but what was she supposed to do next?

I have to go home, she realized with stunning

certainty. She had to get out of the city before she ended up sleeping on a park bench somewhere.

One glance at her watch, however, and her heart plummeted into her boots. It was past midnight. The last bus for Everwood left the city at 11:45. She was entirely stuck.

What is wrong *with me?* Amy wondered, walking over to a city bus stop and plopping down on the cold, metal seat. *Do I not have a brain anymore?*

She had to call someone. She needed help. But it wasn't like she could call her parents—they might not even know she was gone. And besides, her father had just thrown her drive to Wyoming in her face. The last thing she wanted to do was ask him to come pick her up in Denver.

Tommy's cell phone was still off, so that left him out. Who else could she call?

Ephram, she thought, knowing that even though they didn't talk much anymore, he'd be there for her if he could. But she didn't want to spoil his holiday. And who knew? Maybe he was with Madison. She couldn't bust up that particular party without feeling like a pathetic loser.

There was only one person left. Amy pulled out her cell phone and quickly dialed the number. It rang five times before someone fumbled with the phone and picked it up.

"Hello?"

"Grandma?" Amy said. "I kind of need your help."

• • •

"Thanks for not calling my dad," Amy said as she buckled her seatbelt in the front seat of Irv's truck.

"He's not going to be happy about this. You realize that, don't you?" her grandmother said, starting the engine.

"I just want one night with no yelling," Amy said, settling in for the long drive. "Just one night, Grandma. Please?"

Her grandmother looked at her in the dim lights flashing by outside the window of the moving car. Amy could see she was worried about her. It was getting so tiring, everyone looking at her like that all the time. But in this case, it might work to her advantage.

"Okay. We'll go back to my place, you'll get some sleep, and we'll talk to your parents in the morning. How's that sound?" her grandmother said.

Amy closed her eyes and leaned her head back, hoping the swooshing of the tires against the road would lull her to sleep so she could forget this whole miserable day ever happened.

"It sounds great, Grandma," she said. "Thanks."

And a few minutes later, Amy finally dozed off.

That night when his dad got home from Lord knew where, Ephram was waiting for him. He crouched in front of the roaring fire he'd built in the fireplace, the only light in the room. The fire was comforting and warm and the fact that Ephram had gotten it going himself, without his father's help or even his presence, somehow made him feel confident enough to say what he had to say.

"I saw Madison tonight," he told his dad as he walked into the room. "And I'm gonna keep seeing her. And there's nothing you can do to stop me."

Talking to his dad like that made him feel exhilarated and sick all at the same time.

"I know," his father said. "I'm not gonna try."

Ephram sat up a little straighter. This was surprising. He wasn't even sure he could find the words to respond to that one.

"I'm going to let you do this, Ephram. I think it's wrong. I think you're making a big mistake. But I think I have to let you make it," he said.

"Gotta admit, not the direction I thought this conversation was going to go," Ephram said, resisting the urge to jump up and down in shocked joy.

His father pulled a chair over from the dining room table and sat down by the fire, just feet away from Ephram. It still felt like they had miles between them.

"I also want you to know that my concerns about this . . . this—"

"Relationship," Ephram supplied defiantly.

"My concerns have nothing to do with you," his dad said. "Not in the way you think. I know you're not an average sixteen-year-old kid. I've known that for a long time. But that doesn't mean you're ready for something like this. And it doesn't mean that *I'm* ready to watch you go through something like this. But I value what we've been building here too much to risk destroying it by trying to stop you."

Ephram looked into the fire, watching it dance, letting it warm his face.

"And I also know that if I forbid you, it will only make it that much more appealing."

"This isn't some act of rebellion," Ephram said automatically. "This is real, Dad."

"I know it is," his father said. They sat in silence for a moment, both gazing into the fire like it could tell them what to say next. "You should have been honest with me from the beginning," his father said finally.

"I know. And I'm sorry. It just all happened so fast . . . before I thought about it," Ephram told him.

"Yeah," his father said, sounding almost sad. "Life's like that sometimes."

Ephram glanced at his father, not sure of what he was thinking about. His mom? His move to Everwood? All the ways their life had changed in the past year and a half?

But as curious as he was, one thought outweighed all the others: Ephram was going to be with Madison. He had his father's blessing. As awful as this day had started out, it was ending better than he could have ever hoped.

Amy sat in the chair at the end of the coffee table at her grandmother's house the next day, trying to calm her nervously fluttering heart. Her parents were on their way over and they were furious with her. Her grandmother had described the scene at the Abbott house that morning—police cars, FBI agents, a couple of guys tapping the phone. Her parents had practically called in the National Guard when they found Amy missing. They had totally overreacted and now Amy knew they were going to take it out on her.

I just needed to get out of there. He'd threatened to put a bolt on my door, Amy thought, trying to bolster herself for the conversation she was about to have. *What did they expect me to do?*

She was in the right this time. She knew she was. Her father had been awful the night before. And maybe she shouldn't have run out and made them worry, but after the way they had treated her and Tommy, they deserved a little wake-up call. Amy couldn't be pushed around anymore—she couldn't be told what to do. They had to know that.

The doorbell rang and she heard her grandmother saying hello to her parents. Curt, icy words were exchanged and Amy's pulse took it up another notch. She lowered her feet to the floor, then raised them and tucked them under her again. Somehow she couldn't stop fidgeting.

"Amy," her father said as he stepped into the room.

"Hi," she replied.

Her mother said nothing and barely even looked at her. Amy swallowed hard. She never would have expected a colder reception from her mother than from her father. At least she had tried to stop him from attacking Tommy the night before. What had changed since then?

Just stay calm. You know what you're going to say and you know you're right, Amy told herself. *Just take the high road.*

"Well, we're here," her father said as he and her mother sat down on the couch kitty-corner from Amy. "You wanted to talk, so talk."

Amy glanced at her mother, who still hadn't looked at her, and cleared her throat. Her grandmother sat at the other end of the table and shot her an encouraging glance.

"I know I've made a lot of mistakes, and for that, I'm sorry," Amy began. Her parents exchanged a look and finally, *finally* her mother shifted her gaze to Amy. There was hope behind her eyes. A promising start.

"The thing is, I'm doing better," Amy told them. "It may not look like it, but I am. I've been sleeping more, catching up at school. I finally feel like

I'm waking up. And I thought about it, and it all started when I met Tommy."

Her father rolled his eyes. "That's ridiculous. . . ."

"Just hear me out, please," Amy said. She couldn't handle it if he just started interrupting her again and not letting her explain. "He's not a bad person. I know what you heard, but if you took the time to get to know him, you'd see that none of it is true. But the way you treated him at dinner . . . it was humiliating. If you were that worried, you could have talked to me in private. But to bring it up in front of the whole family, not to mention him . . ."

Amy's father blinked and looked at the ground. For a split second she thought he might apologize, but he stayed silent.

"I don't want it to be this way," Amy said. "I don't want to fight all the time."

"Neither do we," her father said.

Amy looked at her mother, who had gone back to staring down at her hands. *Is she going to say anything?* Amy thought.

"I know I said some things I probably shouldn't have, and I wish I could take them back, but I can't," Amy said. "All I can say now is I hope you can forgive me."

There. They had to respect that, right? She was being mature about this—kowtowing and asking for their forgiveness. It was what they wanted. She knew it was.

"The entire episode was a disaster," her father said, a more reasonable tone in his voice. "We all wish it had never happened, and I can see where perhaps I may have overreacted. But now that we've all had time—"

"Do you even realize what you've done?" Amy's mother said without lifting her eyes.

"Rose—"

"I don't think she does," her mother said, her voice quaking with anger. She looked at her husband, then at Amy, and Amy realized she'd never seen this expression on her mother's face. She looked stricken. She looked miserable. She looked *mad*. "Amy, the FBI was at our house. We actually had to consider the possibility that you took your own life. Do you know what that is like for a parent?"

We're being a little melodramatic here, aren't we? Amy thought. "Mom, I said I was sorry."

"No, you didn't," her mother snapped. "Not for lying to us. Not for making us worry like that. And you have the gall to sit there and say *we* embarrassed *you*? How do you think we felt telling Grandma and Pop-Pop you couldn't say good-bye because you ran away?"

Amy pressed her lips together. The venom in her mother's voice was overwhelming.

"*You* are the embarrassment, Amy. Your attitude, your behavior . . . and now you summon us over here, like we've been granted some audience with the Pope? Because you *deign* to talk to us? This is way past self-indulgence."

Amy looked at her grandmother. "See? I can't talk to them."

"You want to be treated like an adult, then *act* like one," her mother said.

"The important thing now is that she comes home," her father said, putting his hands out.

"No. What's important is that she takes responsibility for her actions," her mother interjected.

"Rose," Amy's grandmother said. "I think that's what she's—"

"Don't you *dare* talk to me," Amy's mother said fiercely, shocking all of them. "For twenty-five years I've sat back and watched you treat Harold with disrespect. I never said anything. But this is different. Amy is our daughter. You undermined our authority as parents, betrayed our trust as a family. If anybody needs forgiveness, it's you. And I have to say I don't know if I'll ever be able to give it to you." She turned back to Amy, who was reeling at the rate at which the conversation had deteriorated. "You want to come home, fine. The rules are the same—no car, no telephone, no dating that boy."

"That is so unfair!" Amy blurted out.

"Too bad," her mother said. "I'm tired of giving you the benefit of every doubt. You lost the right to that a long time ago."

"I'm not a kid anymore," Amy said. "I can make my own decisions!"

"That's right," her mother said. "You heard what I said, now you can decide. Come home and live by my rules, or stay here. It's your choice." She stood up, pulling her purse onto her shoulder. "Come on, Harold."

Her dad hesitated for a moment and her mother glared at him.

"I said we're leaving," she said firmly.

Then she turned and walked out, followed by Amy's father. Amy and her grandmother just sat there for a moment, stunned. Amy felt all hollowed out inside. She had tried to do the right thing and it had backfired on her—enormously.

"Well. That went great," she said quietly.

"They'll come around," her grandmother said. "You'll see. And in the meantime you're welcome to stay here."

"Thanks, Grandma," Amy said flatly. She stood up and was surprised to find that her legs were shaky and weak. "I guess I'll just go . . . settle into the guest room."

She walked slowly up the stairs and into the room where she had crashed earlier that morning. The walls were covered in flowered wallpaper, the bookshelves stuffed with old volumes of medical books her grandfather had collected before his death. It was kind of depressing. But apparently it was home.

Amy crawled onto the bed, turned, and sat back against the headboard, going over everything that had just happened in her mind. She had never seen her mother like that before, never imagined she could be so unreasonable. That was her father's job.

How could she sit there and forbid her to see the one person that made her happy? All her parents ever said they wanted was for her to snap out of it—to feel better about herself and her life. Then she had sat there and told her mother that Tommy helped her feel that way and they had still told her she could never see him again.

Was Amy totally insane? This didn't make any sense, did it?

She slid down further on the bed and stared up at the ceiling, knowing that tonight sleep was never going to come. All she was going to do for the next few hours was lay here and wonder where it had all gone wrong.

CHAPTER 7

A beautiful girl. A big couch. An empty house. What more could a guy want out of life? Ephram slipped his arm around Madison and kissed the little spot between her collarbone and her neck. She closed her eyes for a moment, enjoying it, then remembered where she was and whacked the side of his face lightly with the back of her hand.

"Ow!" Ephram protested.

"I thought we were watching a movie," Madison said, staring at the TV screen, legs crossed tightly, arms crossed over her stomach.

"It's on, isn't it?" Ephram asked, trying again.

She pulled back from him, sliding sideways on the couch. "So in your world, 'You wanna come over and watch a movie?' really means . . ."

"'You wanna come over and make out?'" Ephram said matter-of-factly. "And, for the record, it's not just in my world. It's, like, the law of the universe."

He moved in for a real kiss and Madison smiled and playfully pushed him away.

"What?" Ephram said with a laugh.

"We're not allowed to in the house," she said.

"Do I look like a man who follows rules?" he asked, raising his eyebrows. He slipped his hand under her hair and let the long tresses slide over his fingers. "I fly in the face of danger. I bend to no—"

Just then the back door opened and Ephram instantly jumped to the other side of the couch, leaving a good three feet between himself and Madison.

"We're just watching a movie," he said, all innocence.

"I hate you! You're a liar!" Delia shouted.

Ephram and Madison sat up and turned around as his dad closed the door. His father and Delia had gone out to buy a Christmas tree and apparently somehow it had resulted in World War III. What the heck was going on?

"Delia, please," Ephram's father said, his face creased with worry. "I'm sorry. How many times can I apologize?"

"A thousand million billion and I still won't care!" Delia replied, whirling on him. "You promised!"

Ephram and Madison exchanged a look. This was serious stuff, whatever it was.

"It was an accident," Ephram's father said. "I didn't mean to—"

"It wasn't an accident!" Delia accused. "You kissed her. *On the lips!* For, like, ten seconds!"

Kissed her? Kissed who? Ephram thought, glancing at his father, his stomach turning. His dad wasn't supposed to be going around kissing women.

"Hey. What's going on?" Madison asked, her voice full of concern.

"He kissed Linda!" Delia informed her. "On *purpose!*"

Linda . . . Linda Abbott? Oh, this was no good. Delia hated Linda Abbott. But Ephram was seeing his father in a whole new light. He'd actually gotten Linda Abbott to kiss him? The woman was hot—well, for an old person.

I can't believe I just thought that, Ephram scolded himself, his insides hollowing out. What would his mother think?

"Sweetie, listen to me," Ephram's dad said. "I swear I didn't mean for it to happen. Please—"

"You promised!" Delia shouted, her little face splotchy and red. "You promised and you did it anyway. Which makes you a liar!"

"Delia . . ."

But apparently Ephram's sister had had enough.

She turned on her heel and ran out, taking the stairs at record speed. Ephram's father hung his head and Madison sighed as she got up.

"I'll go talk to her," she said, slipping from the room.

Ephram's father came around the couch and sat in Madison's place. Ephram had about a million questions and emotions warring for first place in line, so he did what he always did in such situations. He cracked a joke.

"So, I take it you kissed Linda?" he said.

"Funny," his father replied, sounding spent.

"What did she mean, 'you promised'?" Ephram asked, looking down at his hands.

His father sighed long and slow. "Does it really matter?"

Ephram shot him a look. They both knew that you didn't go back on a promise to Delia. Whatever she was angry about, if his father had betrayed a promise, it made it ten times worse.

"Fine. As it turns out, you were right," his father said. "Delia *was* upset about me and Linda."

Ephram blinked, trying to recall when he'd said this. It had been that night Linda had come by to cook dinner and Delia had said the S-word at the table. It felt like a million years had passed since then.

"That was, like, three months ago," he said. "You catch on quick."

"So I talked to her about it, and I explained that someday I might be interested in a woman—romantically," his father said.

Ugh. Barfworthy, Ephram thought, trying hard not to imagine his father and Linda Abbott making out.

"She said it was fine, as long as it wasn't Linda," his dad finished.

Ephram almost laughed. "Let me get this straight: The night you went up to punish Delia for dropping the *S* bomb, you ended up promising not to date Linda Abbott?"

Ephram's dad looked at him from the corner of his eye. "She's very persuasive."

There was a question that Ephram was dying to ask, but at the same time he wasn't sure he wanted the answer. He thought of his mother, wondered if there really was a heaven, and if so, whether she was looking down on this conversation.

"So . . . are you going to?" he asked awkwardly. "Date her, I mean?"

"I don't know," his father said. "I'd like to, but Delia is so upset. . . . "

What do you think, Ephram? Ephram thought, mentally putting words in his father's mouth. *How would you feel if I dated Linda Abbott?*

He watched his dad and waited for him to ask this most obvious question. When he didn't move or say anything, Ephram felt all the muscles in his body clench. Didn't his father *care* what *he* thought? How *he* felt? Delia wasn't the only kid around here who had lost her mother and had to deal with the idea of her father dating again.

"So? She's ten," he said finally. "Buy her an extra Barbie doll and she'll forget all about the stupid promise."

"I'm not going to bribe your sister," his dad replied.

"Why not? Bribery is your thing," Ephram pointed out. "You promised her a horse so she'd move out here. Which, by the way, you never bought her. Come to think of it, you suck at keeping promises."

"You're not helping," his dad said.

"So what are you going to do?" Ephram asked.

"Well, I might not have to do anything," his dad answered. "After today's nightmare, I doubt Linda Abbott would want anything to do with me."

"Great," Ephram said. "Problem solved."

That would be the perfect solution—if this all just went away. Clearly none of them was ready to deal with it yet. Ephram knew for sure that *he* wasn't—his stomach felt like it was expanding and contracting over and over and over again.

"So," Ephram said, ready for a subject change. He looked around and clasped his hands together. "Where's the tree?"

His father hung his head a little farther. Ephram

knew it was one of those moments when he felt like he couldn't get anything right. And while his heart went out to his dad, it was kind of comforting to know that he wasn't the only one who had such moments. Even perfect Dr. Brown messed up occasionally.

The following weekend Ephram sat in the living room alone with Madison, removing Chinese-food boxes from the greasy-bottomed bags they'd arrived in. His father was off on a bonding camping trip with Delia, trying to make up with her for the fact that he was dating Linda Abbott—or thinking about dating her. Meanwhile Ephram had been left behind with no one trying to bond with him or make anything up to him at all.

Not that he cared. Really. He was a big boy. He could handle it.

He pulled a box out and popped it open, then dropped it on the table top and exhaled loudly.

"What is this? I didn't order this," he said.

"I'm not really hungry yet," Madison said, reaching her arm behind him. "Maybe we should 'watch a movie' for a while first." She rested her chin on his shoulder and looked up at him seductively.

Ephram barely even noticed. "I said moo shu *chicken*," he said, throwing a hand out in frustration. Why was the whole world against him? "This is pork. I don't eat pork. I'm gonna call them. . . ."

He started to stand up, but Madison stopped him with a hand to his arm. "Ephram, do we have to do this now?" she asked.

"You're right. By the time they switch it, the rest of the food will be cold," he said, irritated. He sat back down and collapsed deeper into the couch. "This sucks!"

Madison leaned back from him and tilted her head. Clearly it was starting to dawn on her that Ephram wasn't really upset about the Chinese food. Not entirely, anyway.

"Okay, what's bugging you?" she asked, crossing her arms over her chest. "And don't tell me it's the moo shu, because no amount of unwanted pork should distract you from pushing for another make-out session. Especially when there's no possibility of getting caught."

"I wouldn't count on that," Ephram said, wanting to avoid the subject of his repressed anger. "I doubt my dad will be able to deal with my sister *and* nature for an entire night. They'll be home. Trust me."

"Why do you say that?" Madison asked.

"'Cause I know my father," Ephram said. "The man has zero communication skills. I mean, he's better with Delia, but—"

Ephram snapped his mouth shut, sensing from Madison's suddenly comprehending expression that he had said too much. He turned away and busied himself with reorganizing the food cartons in front of him. Classic diversion tactic.

"Did he talk to you at all about Linda?" Madison asked gently.

"What about her?" Ephram asked, going for stoic.

"About his dating her," she said. "I mean, he planned this whole trip with your sister, I assumed . . ."

"Delia's a kid. She doesn't get it yet," Ephram said, regurgitating the mantra he'd been trying to convince himself of. He was a guy. He understood. His dad needed some lovin', needed to move on. The only problem was, he *didn't* understand. Not entirely. His mom had been gone for less than two years. It seemed way too soon for dating.

"And you do?" Madison asked.

"Don't start," Ephram said, tensing up. If she was going to start talking down to him because of their age difference he was going to have to die.

"This isn't about your age. This is about your father dating for the first time since your mom died," Madison said, trying to get Ephram to look her in the eye by putting herself directly in front of him. "You're not supposed to just 'get it.' You're supposed to talk about it."

"Nothing to talk about," he said.

He grabbed the remote and turned on the TV. Conversation over, or so he thought.

"You know, I hated every guy my mom brought home after the divorce," Madison said.

Ephram looked down, a lump forming in his throat. He knew she was trying to sympathize—trying to make him feel like he wasn't the only person this had happened to—but she had no idea how he felt. She couldn't possibly.

"My dad's not divorced," he said.

"Oh, God. I know, Ephram," Madison said. "I'm sorry, that came out wrong."

"Look, it's no big deal," Ephram said. "I didn't think he'd start dating so soon. He did. It's weird. I'm over it."

"Your dad goes on a date for the first time in your entire life, doesn't ask how you feel about it, and you've emotionally processed the experience in under thirty seconds. Impressive," Madison said with a nod.

"What do you want from me?" Ephram snapped, turning his palms up. "I'm not gonna tell my dad how to live his life. If he's ready, then I should be too."

Madison reached over and took Ephram's hand in both of hers. There had never been a more comforting gesture. Just her touch made his tension ease a bit, like his muscles were exhaling.

"Here's the thing: You can be *not* okay with it and still support your dad's decision," she said. "And if you feel like you can talk to him about it, then you should. But if you can't . . . talk to me, 'cause chances are, if I know you're feeling gloomy, I'll do stuff to cheer you up."

Ephram smiled. It was good to have a girlfriend. He sat back, squeezed her hand, and looked her in the eye.

"This is good," he said. "Just . . . this."

Madison smiled and nodded and they cuddled into the couch together to actually watch a movie.

Ephram dropped his reheated pizza slice and looked out the kitchen window when he heard his father's SUV pull up on Sunday night. Both Delia and his dad were smiling when they got out of the car, which he took as a good sign. Ephram still couldn't believe they hadn't given up and come home early. But maybe his father had been right about the camping trip idea all along. It appeared to have done the trick, at least.

The door opened and Delia came bounding in, ran right over to Ephram and hugged him around the waist.

"I love you, Ephram," she said, smiling up at him.

Ephram smirked, half-moved, half-disturbed. "I love you too, Delia," he said.

Then she grabbed her bag and ran upstairs. His father closed the door and dropped the camping equipment on the floor, looking very pleased with himself.

"What did you guys do up there, join a cult or something?" Ephram asked.

"No. Your sister has just decided to spread the love," his father replied. "Oddly enough, I think it was something I said that brought this on."

"Wow. So camping was a success," Ephram said, sitting at the counter again and taking a bite out of his pizza. He couldn't help but feel a slight jealous twinge. Clearly his sister and his father had made up, had a heart-to-heart, gotten all square with the Linda thing. Ephram almost wished he had gone with them. He wouldn't mind feeling as happy and lighthearted as his sister seemed at the moment.

"The camping, no. The father-daughter thing, yes," his dad said, joining him in the kitchen.

"You ended up in a hotel, didn't you?" Ephram said.

"With a minibar," his father confirmed.

"Bribery will get you everywhere."

"Not exactly. As it turns out your sister was just worried that if she opened her heart to another woman, your mom would be mad at her," his father said.

"Kids," Ephram said dismissively, though he'd been feeling almost exactly the same thing.

"I told her your mom would never be mad at any of us for liking someone new," he said, the self-satisfied smile still present. "That she would want your sister to love as much as possible."

Ephram raised his eyebrows. "Can't wait to see her throw that back in your face when she starts dating."

His father's face finally fell.

"Just kidding," Ephram said, getting up and dumping the rest of his pizza in the trash.

"You'd better be," his dad replied.

Ephram grabbed his soda can, the better to fortify himself for that pesky homework he'd neglected to do all weekend long, and headed for the stairs.

"So, listen. There's something I need to do and I was hoping you would come with me," his father said.

Ephram paused. Was this it? Was his father finally going to give Ephram the chance to voice his feelings about Linda? Much to Ephram's chagrin, his heart actually started to pound a little harder. The very idea of having this conversation made him beyond nervous.

"I have this patient . . . Helen. Her husband, Stan, passed away a few years back, and before he did, they had some of his sperm frozen so that Helen could, if she wished, have his baby one day," his father explained.

It took a moment for this new and wildly unexpected information to compute in Ephram's mind. *Okay . . . So this has nothing to do with me. Or Linda. Or how I feel about the whole thing. This has to do with some dead guy's sperm?*

His father looked at him expectantly, waiting for Ephram to react.

"Okay . . . ," Ephram said.

"Well, Helen's remarried and she and her new husband want to have a baby, so she's decided to give up on the idea of carrying Stan's."

"What's this have to do with me?" Ephram asked.

"Helen has asked me to . . . dispose of Stan's sperm," his father said.

"Why don't I like the direction this conversation is going?" Ephram asked.

"No. It's nothing weird. It's just, she wants me to toss it from this hiker's overlook. Apparently it was one of Stan's favorite places," his father said. "But it's kind of a long hike to do alone."

Ephram blinked. "So you want me to go on a hike with you to hurl some dead guy's sperm into the mountains?"

"Basically," his father said.

Ephram's dad had gotten some strange medical cases since coming to Everwood. He'd fielded some freakish questions and odd requests. But this, hands down, had to be the strangest.

Delia gets a bonding trip to a hotel (plus minibar) and I get the most bizarre day trip of the century, Ephram thought. But then it hit him. This was his opportunity. If his father was never going to ask him what he thought about this thing with Linda, then Ephram would just tell him. And a hike alone in the mountains seemed like the perfect time to do it. Ephram was going to take charge.

"I'm there," Ephram said.

And so Ephram found himself, on a cold December day, hiking up a mountain with his father who was carrying a thermos full of sperm.

At least it would be a funny story to tell one day.

"I think I'm getting a nosebleed," Ephram said.

"We're here," his dad replied, checking a piece of paper against the elevation marker near the edge of the overlook. "This is the spot."

"Good, 'cause I think I'm dying," Ephram said, catching his breath.

"Don't forget we've still got to walk back down," his father told him, smiling.

"Nah. Think I'll just live here," Ephram replied. "Send up some pizza when you get back to town."

His father looked out over the canyon and let out a long breath. "Peaceful, isn't it?"

"Yeah. It's good," Ephram said. The mountain peaks were all white and gray and the clouds were high against the bright blue sky. The view definitely didn't suck.

"So, this was Stan's favorite place," his father said. "Pretty easy to see why."

He reached into his backpack and pulled out the silver thermoslike container that held this Stan's frozen sperm. Ephram couldn't stop staring at it. This whole thing was just so weird.

"Isn't there some kind of law against dumping sperm in a national forest?" Ephram joked.

"Probably," his father responded.

"Your job is getting really strange."

"You kidding? I used to drill holes into people's heads for a living. This is cake," his father said.

Ephram looked at his dad, smiling there like everything was fine, and he realized that it was now or never. All the way up to the mountain he had avoided broaching the Linda subject with his dad, blaming the lack of conversation on all the gasping-for-air. But he knew now that he couldn't have asked for a more perfect place to do this. They were together. They were alone. And no one was going to be disturbing them, that was for sure.

"Before we do this, I need to talk," he said.

Out of the corner of his eye he saw his father look at him, surprised, but Ephram stared straight ahead, out over the amazing mountains in front of him.

"You mean *we* need to talk, or—"

"No. Just me," Ephram said. He took a deep breath and let it rip. "I like Linda. I can see why *you* like her too. I think. But . . . I'm not as cool with you starting to date as you probably want me to be. It's not that I'm *not* cool with it, I just . . . the fact is, it's weird. In some part of my brain, I guess I thought you'd turn into one of those happy widowers who has a lot of old lady friends and pets, kinda like Andy Griffith."

His father looked at him, shocked again, and Ephram shrugged. "Nick at Nite," he explained.

His dad nodded and Ephram continued.

"But that's not you, and I know that now," he said. "And I want you to be happy. So if dating Linda is going to make you happy, then I'll find a way to feel less weird about it. It may take some time, but I'm willing to try. There. I'm done. We can throw the sperm now."

Ephram, at this point, pretty much felt like he could fly. He had said everything he was feeling and it had all come out sounding kind of okay—kind of adult and not whiny. Now all he could do was hope his dad didn't say anything to screw up the moment.

"You wanna do the honors?" he asked, holding out the canister. A perfect response.

"Cool," Ephram said.

He took the canister, pulled back, and launched it out into open space as far as he possibly could. The physical exertion of the toss, following the emotional exertion of the speech, was cathartic. The thermos flipped over a few times and smacked into the evergreen branches down below.

CHAPTER 8

Ephram had said his piece about Linda. He wasn't a hundred percent okay with the fact that his dad was dating, but he had accepted that it was going to happen and that was about all he could do. His father had also said *his* piece about Ephram dating Madison, had accepted that it was going to happen, and had realized that this was about all he could do. What Ephram had yet to figure out was whether Madison was okay with dating *him*. It seemed like they barely ever went out in public and when they did she walked about four feet away from him. Ephram understood that on some level she was afraid of people realizing they were breaking the law, but it wasn't like every single person on the street was watching them, cell phone in hand, ready to call the police. At this point Ephram would have killed to just hold the girl's hand for two seconds in the open air.

But instead he was jogging behind her as they crossed the street in Morrisville, a town half an hour outside of Everwood, headed for the movie theater. Thanks to an accident on the one road that connected the two towns, they were fifteen minutes behind schedule.

"We made it," Madison said, checking her watch.

"Barely," Ephram replied. "You know if you'd let me take you to the movie theater in town instead of worrying about who was gonna see us—"

"You wanna fight about this again or do you want to see a movie?" Madison asked over her shoulder.

"Little bit of both," Ephram said as they joined the line outside the ticket booth. He checked the clock on the wall behind the ticket guy. "Okay, we have exactly enough time to make the movie if we divide and conquer."

"You get tickets, I'll pick snacks," Madison said.

"Why do you get to pick snacks?" Ephram asked.

"Because you have this weird thing against fake butter," she replied, smacking him on the back. "Go. Buy."

Madison jogged inside and over to the concession line as Ephram stepped up to the counter. The poor sap behind the glass was dressed in a white shirt, black bow tie, and red vest. He was probably about Madison's age, and probably ruing the day he'd taken a job that forced him to sit in a cage every Saturday night watching other people having fun.

Of course, that was hardly Ephram's problem. He was out with his hot girlfriend. And now that they were here and they were on time, he could relax.

"Can I get two for *The Last Samurai*?" Ephram asked.

The ticket guy printed the passes out and was about to slide them over, when he took a look at Ephram. He paused.

"Hold it," he said. "I'm going to need to see some ID, please."

"Since when?" Ephram asked.

"Since 1968, when the Motion Picture Association of America said that no one under seventeen can be admitted to an R-rated film without a parent or guardian," the guy said, drunk with power.

Please don't make my life miserable just because yours is, Ephram thought. "I've been seeing R-rated movies since I was born, so I was grandfathered in, I assure you," he shot back.

"There's an 8:15 showing of the *Rugrats* rerelease if you want," the guy said, enjoying the conflict a bit too much. "Plenty of seats."

Ephram glanced behind the guy into the lobby and saw Madison paying for the food. There was little time to spare. Clearly he was going to have to take a different approach.

"I don't know how to explain this in the little time I have, but this is very, very, *very* important," he said, his heart pounding in anticipation of total humiliation.

The guy just looked at him.

"I'm on a date, and that's kind of a rare thing for me. You look like a guy who can appreciate that . . ."

Now the vendor just looked at him with serious fire in his eyes. *Nice one, idiot,* Ephram thought.

"Not that you don't look like you get a lot of action or whatever," he babbled. "I'll bet you do."

Oh, God! She was practically right on top of them now.

"Look, you gotta let me in. The money's right there. Keep the change."

Madison stepped up next to Ephram, her arms loaded down with food, just as the ticket guy looked past Ephram's left shoulder at the guy behind him.

"Next!"

"I thought I'd compromise, so I took the butter on the side in a cup, which, as it turns out, is actually vile," Madison said, all chipper. "Did you get the tickets?"

Ephram's throat was closed off with total mortification. He couldn't have spoken if he tried. He'd spent half his time with Madison trying to convince her that the age difference meant nothing, only to have this thrown in his face—he couldn't even go to a real movie without his daddy. This couldn't be happening to him. It was just too, too awful.

Madison glanced at the ticket guy and stepped up to the window, placing the popcorn on the counter.

"Can I have two for *Samurai*?" she asked.

Somebody just shoot me now, Ephram thought, his face burning.

"Are you over seventeen?" the guy asked.

Madison whipped out her wallet and slapped it open against the glass, showing her license. It would have been kind of cool if she was saving someone else's ass, but Ephram was still hoping for sudden death.

"And are you this boy's parent or legal guardian?" the guy asked, all cocky, already knowing, per Ephram, that she was not.

Madison turned her head and glanced at him and the pity and embarrassment on her face were too much to take.

Mental note, he thought morosely, *next time, I'm in charge of food.*

It was one of those crucial moments in a relationship. Even someone with a relationship track record as nonexistent as Ephram's recognized this. If he wanted to keep Madison around, he was going to have to do something and he was going to have to do something fast. Things could not go on the way they were. It was time to go on the offensive.

When he came home from school on Wednesday afternoon to find Madison on the couch highlighting a textbook and Delia nowhere to be scene, he decided to take the bull by the horns. He plopped down right next to her and Madison looked up from her book.

"How much time do we spend together?" Ephram asked, dropping his backpack at his feet.

"A lot," she said in a suspicious tone.

"How much fun is that?" he asked.

"A lot," she said, capping her highlighter as she sensed this was going somewhere.

"Good answer. Now here's the tough one," Ephram said. "How many times have we had fun outside the confines of my father's property?"

Madison blinked. "Not a lot," she said.

"Try again."

"Never," she said, resigned.

Ephram nodded and turned to face her on the couch, drawing one leg up underneath him.

"We're great. We like the same bad movies. . . . You laugh at my dumb jokes. . . . You even pretended to like my dumb comics and don't think I didn't appreciate that," he said. "We're great so long as we stay in the bubble and you keep me out of sight. Which has its charm. But we've been at this for six weeks and I haven't even met your roommate."

"She's a total bitch," Madison said.

"If we're going to be anything more than two people who watch movies and make out in an ugly car four afternoons a week, you've got to get over it," he said.

"I guess I'm not holding up my end, being the mature one in the relationship," Madison said, biting her lip. "I'm sorry about the other day at the movie theater. I should've said something to that guy."

"Trust me. If you had, it would've been worse," Ephram said. "But what sucked was the way you bum rushed me outta there after that like you were afraid to be caught with the kindergartener."

Madison looked down and Ephram could see he'd gotten to her.

"Come out with me Friday night," he said. "There's this wrestling thing that's apparently can't-miss. Downside is it's in public. Consider it an experiment. An hour there, then straight back to the bubble."

Madison's brow wrinkled as she eyed him dubiously. "At County?" she said. "I swore once I graduated I'd never walk those halls again."

Ephram's stomach turned. She couldn't be shooting him down. Not after all the planning of the offensive.

"Then again, I am breaking the law dating

you. What's one promise?" she said with a smile. "Sounds swell."

Ephram's whole face lit up. "Really?"

Madison narrowed her eyes. "Go do your homework. I have to study."

Ephram planted a quick kiss on her lips, then got up and grabbed his book bag, hightailing it up to his room before she could change her mind. He was going to the wrestling meet with Madison— Madison and him, out in front of all the kids at school.

Huh. Maybe they wouldn't pick on his car so much after this. It was about time Ephram Brown got a little respect around County High.

R-E-S-P-E-C-T! Find out what it means to me. R-E-S-P-E-C-T. Take care, TCB.

Amy stared at herself in the scratched mirror in the third-floor bathroom at County. For some reason the stupid old song "Respect" was playing itself over and over in her head. Probably because she couldn't seem to get any respect. Not anymore, anyway.

"This is so annoying," she muttered to herself, digging through her bag for a hairbrush. She was so clenched and tense her hand was shaking. "I don't even know what that stupid line means. What the heck is TCB?"

She took a deep breath and let it out slowly,

trying to calm her frayed nerves. Things had been bad at school lately, what with her friends talking about her behind her back and people who used to smile and greet her suddenly avoiding her at all costs. But today it had gotten even worse. Today everywhere Amy went people were whispering and throwing her looks. Today someone had even grimaced when she walked by. Why was today different? Because Crystal Leonard had spotted Amy and Tommy at Sal's Pizza over the weekend and now the entire student body knew that the former homecoming queen was now dating the druggie who tried to burn down the school.

In a small town like Everwood there was no better fodder for gossip than a fallen homecoming queen.

That was why Amy was using the third-floor bathroom that smelled like skunk and had two broken toilets. The bathroom no one in the school ever used. At least there she was safe from all the talk.

"Who cares what they think?" she whispered to herself as she pulled her brush through her long hair. "You know how great Tommy is. If they don't want to see it, that's their problem."

She dropped her brush back in her bag and looked into her own sad eyes. Unfortunately, no matter how many times she gave herself that pep talk, it still felt in her heart like it was *her* problem.

She still had to go to school all day, every day. She still had to hear the words and see the looks. And on top of it all, she had to worry about bumping into Bright and how he would treat her now that she had moved out. Put it all together and Amy Abbott was one on-edge girl.

She checked her watch and threw her bag onto her shoulder. Only three more classes and then she was outta there. She would meet Tommy at the drugstore and everything would be fine. When she was around Tommy, she always felt calmer— except when they were walking past her dad's office or Town Hall where her mom worked. In those cases she always quickened her steps. Amy didn't know what she was going to do the first time she and Tommy crossed paths with her parents.

"Amy!" Laynie called the second she stepped out of the bathroom. Her doe eyes widened and she looked toward the bathroom in disgust. "Why're you using the skunk room?"

"What're you doing on the third floor?" Amy replied.

"I just walked Danny to art class," Laynie said, grinning giddily.

"Danny? What happened to Bobby?" Amy asked as they headed for the stairs.

"Oh, that totally ended," Laynie said. "Of course he doesn't know it yet, but he will—after I call him tonight."

"Gotcha," Amy said.

"So you didn't answer my question. Why were you using the skunk room?" Laynie asked as they pushed open the door to the stairwell.

"What's the big deal? It's just a bathroom," Amy replied, her body temperature rising as a group of girls tromped by her up the stairs, glancing over their shoulders at her and giggling.

"It is not *just* a bathroom. No one uses the skunk room," Laynie said. "Well, except the burnouts and that's just for smoking—"

Page and Kayla walked by and Amy attempted to smile, but they just ducked their heads together and kept talking as they scurried away.

"I was in the skunk room because whenever I walk into one of the regular bathrooms I get to overhear people talking about me," Amy blurted out, whirling on Laynie.

Her friend stopped, her whole face falling. "Like who?" she asked.

"Like everyone," Amy replied. "Don't tell me you haven't heard it. All anyone's talking about is how I'm dating a druggie and I'm not living at home anymore. I think the football team has a pool going as to whether or not I'm going to OD this year."

"Amy, those guys are morons," Laynie said.

"Yeah, but about two seconds ago they were my friends," Amy replied.

"So? Who needs them?" Laynie replied, hooking her arm through Amy's and starting down the hall again.

I do, Amy thought. *Why is my life so completely different? I lost Colin. Did I really have to lose everyone else, as well?* It wasn't like she had done something wrong. She had lost the love of her life and people were treating her like she'd called in a bomb threat or something. People who lost a loved one were supposed to get sympathy, not be relegated to total outcast status. Maybe she had been a little depressed, but her friends should be able to understand that, right?

"You've got me," Laynie said. "And Danny. And Danny has this really cool friend Corey who you would just love—"

"Are you even listening to me?" Amy said, pulling away. "I'm with Tommy now."

"Well, it's not like you're married," Laynie said, her brow furrowing.

Amy threw up her hands. "Well, maybe I just can't juggle guys as well as you can, all right?"

"What's that supposed to mean?" Laynie asked, crossing her arms over her chest.

"It means all you care about anymore are guys," Amy said. "There are other things in life, Laynie."

"Well, correct me if I'm wrong, but didn't you choose a *guy* over your own family?" Laynie asked.

Amy's heart dropped. She had no response to

that. Essentially, she had done just that. But it was so much more complex than Laynie knew. And just then, Amy had neither the desire nor the energy to try to explain it.

"I have to get to class," she said, turning on her heel.

"Me too," Laynie replied.

They both stalked off. Just as Amy arrived at the end of the hallway, the bell rang, long and loud. Perfect. She was going to be late for class—again. Couldn't she get anything right?

"So, you all ready for the big wrestling tournament?" Tommy asked Amy that night as she lay on her stomach at her grandmother's, pretending to go over some homework. "Rah, rah, County," he added dryly.

Amy appreciated the fact that Tommy was willing to go with her to the big school event, but it was pretty much the last thing she wanted to do after the day she'd had. Walking into County with the evil Tommy Callahan would just make Monday ten times worse. She wasn't ashamed of Tommy, because she knew what an amazing guy he really was. She just didn't want to deal with all the backlash.

"Let's just drop the wrestling meet, okay?" Amy asked, doodling in the margin of her notebook.

"You're the one who wanted to go," Tommy said.

"Now I'm the one who doesn't," Amy replied, glancing at him over her shoulder. He stood in the corner of the guest room, looking confused. Not that Amy could blame him. It had taken her a good half hour of wheedling earlier in the week just to convince him to go. Now she was backing out. "Let's just go for a drive or something."

"Come on, I haven't been to County since they threw me out," Tommy said. "It could be kind of cool. And I thought everyone in school was going to the meet."

Amy dropped her pen and sat up to face Tommy. "That's kind of the problem," she said morosely.

"Your brother will be there," Tommy said, understanding dawning in his eyes. "He's still being an ass?"

"He plays to his strengths," Amy said lightly, even though her heart felt heavy as stone.

"I'll tell you what. I'm fine blowing this off if you want, but you can't keep ducking every time you see the guy," Tommy said. He crouched at the foot of the bed and took Amy's hands, looking into her eyes. "We'll go for an hour. You don't like it, we're back here making out by *Seinfeld*."

Amy couldn't pass up an offer like that. And maybe it would be good to show all her former friends that she didn't care what they thought— that they couldn't make her hide her relationship.

She smiled, leaned forward, and gave Tommy a

quick kiss. It really was amazing the way he made everything seem possible.

Amy didn't even notice the stares as she and Tommy walked in front of the jam-packed bleachers in the County High gym. By the time she and Tommy were seated next to each other, their thighs touching, his hand over hers, she was smiling. With Tommy around, Amy felt insulated. Maybe this wrestling match thing would even be fun.

Or not.

Suddenly Amy saw Ephram walking along the gym floor—and he wasn't alone. He was with Madison. That beautiful, older, seemingly perfect girl. The anti-Amy. At least, the anti-new-Amy.

Oh, God. They're coming over here, Amy thought as the couple left Señor Walker, the Spanish teacher, behind and started up the bleachers. *I so don't want to have this conversation.*

She wasn't jealous of Madison. Not really. But it was a little weird seeing Ephram with another girl. Especially with another girl he looked at the way he was looking at Madison. It was kind of the way he used to look at Amy—yet another thing that had completely changed.

As Ephram took one step at a time, searching for a seat, Amy knew his eyes were going to fall on her at any second. Each moment was like pure anticipatory torture. Finally she couldn't take it anymore. Maybe if she said hello first, she could get through this whole thing faster.

"Ephram," she said, stopping him and his date at the end of her bleacher. He looked at her, looked at Tommy, registered surprise, but recovered quickly. "You came," Amy said.

"I did," Ephram replied. "Y'know. School spirit. Rah."

Amy smiled at how similar his comment was to Tommy's earlier one. *Oh, right. Tommy.* "I don't know if you've ever met," Amy said, glancing at her date. "Ephram, this is Tommy. Tommy, Ephram."

"Hey," Ephram said, lifting his chin in that way guys did.

"How you doin', man," Tommy replied, with equal manly coolness.

There was a moment of silence that couldn't have been more awkward if Bright had come walking up to tell Amy that her parents were officially disowning her.

"You met Madison, right?" Ephram asked, reaching out and slipping his fingers through his date's.

Madison flinched and Amy's heart went out to both of them. She wasn't sure what the deal was, but clearly something was going on. They were both as stiff as boards.

"Yeah, once," Amy said with a smile, trying to ease the tension. "You two find seats yet?"

"We were just looking," Ephram replied.

"There are a couple of extra over here," Amy offered.

"No thanks. We're probably not staying that long," Ephram said, lifting Madison's hand. "Gotta get her back to campus."

Madison's jaw dropped as if she was offended and Amy looked at Ephram. What the heck was he doing? Trying to show the girl off? Amy had told Ephram herself that she wanted him to find a great girl—someone worthy of him. He didn't have to rub it in her face. Every time Amy thought she had a mature relationship with someone, that person seemed to prove her wrong in a heinous fashion.

"Not long at all, actually," Madison said. She yanked her hand back and started up the bleachers again, obviously angry. Apparently Amy wasn't the only one noting Ephram's immature behavior.

Embarrassed, Ephram glanced at Amy, hung his head, and followed after Madison. Amy didn't envy the conversation he was going to be having later.

Well that wasn't too awful, Amy thought sarcastically. What had she been thinking coming here tonight? Apparently only bad things could happen at County.

"'Member how you said we could leave if this sucked?" Amy asked Tommy, picking up her scarf.

"'Bout that time?" Tommy asked.

"Oh yeah," Amy said.

Tommy got up, took Amy's hand, and led her

down the bleachers. They couldn't get out of the gym fast enough.

The instant they hit the main corridor, Amy saw Bright standing by the cheerleaders' fundraising table. He caught one glimpse of her and Tommy, pulled a face, and turned his back on them. Amy's heart hit the floor. Why was her brother doing this to her?

Part of her just wanted to slink away, but she couldn't do that. Amy hadn't done anything to Bright and she couldn't stand the way things were between them. He had to listen to reason.

"Be right back," she said to Tommy. Then she walked over to the table and stepped up next to Bright. He took one look at her and rolled his eyes.

"Come on, Bright. Just let it go," she said.

"What do you want from me, Amy?" he said with more venom than necessary.

"Just tell me how you're doing. You're allowed to do that, right?" Amy said. "I heard you got one of the highest math grades in your class. That's great."

"Yeah. It's great," he said sarcastically.

"I get it. You're mad," Amy said, frustrated. "You don't have to keep doing this. Just talk to me."

"I've got nothing to say," Bright replied. "Go talk to your crackhead boyfriend."

"Tommy's not like that," Amy said, wishing *someone* would just listen to her on this account. "He's a good guy."

"Says you," Bright said.

Oh, how very mature, Amy thought. "Believe what you want about him, but I didn't want to leave home. I tried to compromise. You saw what Mom and Dad did. It was their call."

"You had your chance and you picked him over us," Bright said, irritated. "And now you want to blame them for kicking you out? You have no idea what you did to them when you left. It's like you're giving up everything you used to care about. It's Colin all over again."

Amy felt like he'd just shot her straight through the heart. It was a low blow bringing up Colin. Tears stung her eyes and Amy turned and walked away, brushing right by Tommy and heading for the bathroom. She couldn't believe Bright had said that to her.

Amy found the bathroom mercifully empty. She ducked into a stall to blow her nose and wipe her eyes.

Don't let him get to you, she told herself as she calmly reapplied her lipstick in the mirror. *He's just being a jerk. Typical Bright stuff. You can handle it.*

Looking more confident than she felt inside, Amy fanned her hair over her shoulders and stepped out of the bathroom.

The instant Amy hit the corridor, she knew something was wrong. Sounds of a scuffle echoed off the cinderblock walls and a couple of guys jogged by her toward the main hall. Amy came around the corner and she felt like the floor had been yanked out from under her. She was just in time to see Bright slam Tommy backward into a wall.

"Bright! What are you doing?!" Amy shouted, running toward them. Before she could get to them, Señor Walker came out of the gym and grabbed Bright's arm.

"Quit it! Guys! Stop!" the teacher shouted, somehow managing to pull Bright back.

"Bright, come with me," he said, as Bright yanked himself free. "Let's go, now!" the teacher added. Bright shot Tommy one last pissed-off look, then reluctantly followed the teacher down the hallway. Amy knelt down to help Tommy up. His lip was bleeding and his face was all red from being hit.

"Are you okay?" she asked.

"I'm fine," he replied.

Amy looked up after Bright, her heart splitting in two. He must really hate her to do something like this. Clearly he didn't understand where Amy was coming from, and clearly he wasn't even going to try.

"Come on," Amy said, taking Tommy's arm as he stood. "Let's get out of here."

She ducked her head as the cheerleaders, teachers, and other students that had gathered to witness the fight watched her go. Perfect—more fodder for gossip.

Apparently the world wasn't ready for Amy Abbott and Tommy Callahan.

It was do or die time. After the wrestling match, Madison had asked Ephram to drive her home and neither one of them had said a word the entire trip. Ephram had wanted to apologize, but the words kept getting caught in his throat. Because as much as he wanted to say he was sorry, he also wanted to yell at her. All he'd done was hold her hand. He had held his girlfriend's hand and he was getting the silent treatment for it. That just did not seem fair.

Why was she so ashamed of him? Why was she so afraid to let people know how they felt about each other? Maybe she should be apologizing to him. And so he said nothing.

Three days later, they still hadn't spoken. Ephram realized that if he didn't do something and do it fast, he was going to lose Madison forever. And as upset as he was with her, he wasn't blind to the fact that his actions had been worse than hers. He had promised her he would be cool—that it wouldn't be an immature high school experience, and that was exactly what he had turned it into. There was going to have to be a grand romantic gesture. Of course, on his budget and in a town like Everwood, such things were hard to come by.

So he did the best he could.

When Madison came home from class on Tuesday afternoon, Ephram was waiting outside her little off-campus house with a pizza. Madison saw him from a few yards away and seemed reluctant to approach. But what else could she do? She did live there, after all.

"I thought I'd skip the saga of unreturned phone calls and just ambush you," Ephram began.

"With pizza?" she asked, looking none-too-happy. She wasn't ready to forgive him—yet.

"Well, you can't eat flowers," Ephram said. "This is the more practical peace offering."

Madison stopped just short of rolling her eyes. "You have a lot to learn," she said, brushing by him.

Ephram smiled when he heard her stop in her tracks. She'd seen the flowers he'd left standing on the doorstep. Mission accomplished.

"I'm a quick study," he said, turning around. Madison slowly shifted to face him. "Look, I have a feeling I screwed up," he said. "Just wanted to be sure."

"Be sure," Madison told him, causing his heart to squeeze.

Ephram glanced at the ground for a moment, searching for words. He should have planned out a speech, but the flowers and pizza bit had used up most of his creative romantic energies for the week.

"I'm not gonna defend what was stupid," he said. "I'll just say sorry and mean it and stick with it. I just wanted to introduce you to my world."

"You weren't introducing me. You were using me and flaunting me and it was embarrassing and adolescent and exactly like you said it wouldn't be."

Okay. She had him there.

"I just . . . I don't want our lives to be completely separate anymore," Ephram said. "We've been cooped up for weeks, keeping us a secret, and all I wanna do is shout your name from the rooftops."

"Please don't," Madison said, but actually cracked a smile.

"Rooftops are pretty low in mountain towns anyway," Ephram replied. "It's a lot more dramatic in New York."

Madison's smile widened. She tried to squelch it, but it was too late. Ephram had seen his opening. When she walked over to the steps and sat down, he followed and took a seat next to her.

"If you'd rather I liked you less, tell me," he said. "We could go either way at this point. It'd help to know if you're ready to be okay with us."

Ephram held his breath as he waited for her to answer.

"I am ready to be okay with us," she said, then glanced down. "But . . ."

Ephram swallowed hard. "But."

"I'm not ready for other people not to be okay

with us," Madison told him, looking into his eyes beseechingly. "I don't hide you because you're a constant embarrassment; I hide you because even if it doesn't feel like it, we're doing something wrong."

"We can't stay in the bubble forever," Ephram told her. "The bubble isn't even that safe. Bubbles can pop, or burn down. Someone could rob the bubble."

Madison laughed, then pressed her lips together and looked him in the eye. "How about we figure us out first, before we force ourselves on the world?"

It wasn't the answer Ephram had been looking for, but he understood her fears. And he cared about her enough to want to help her allay them. For now, their bubble would have to do.

"All right," he said, "but can we please kiss and make up now? Because I'm on the clock."

Madison smiled and Ephram leaned in toward her, but she pulled back. "Inside," she said, tipping her head toward the door.

She picked up her flowers, unlocked the door, and pulled him into the house. And for the moment, the bubble was just fine. It was, in fact, perfect.

CHAPTER 9

From that moment on, Ephram was consumed by Madison. Before, he may have been called preoccupied. Possibly even obsessed. But suddenly his world went from being seventy, maybe eighty percent about Madison to being one hundred percent, unequivocally Madison-focused, which would have been okay if he could see her during the day—if he could have lunch with her, hold her hand in the hallway, meet up with her after classes. But he couldn't. He could only see her at home in the afternoons, and even then, kissing was verboten, touching frowned upon. They couldn't go out in public; they could barely find time to be together in private. Ephram had these overwhelming, expansive emotions and there was no place to put them.

And so he wrote a song. He wrote pages and

pages and pages. He wrote for days. He wrote before school, after school, during study hall. If they awarded a Grammy for sheer volume of pages produced, Ephram would have won hands down.

Then, finally, after days of working, Ephram decided it was time to show her. To play for her what he had written—the notes she had inspired. While Delia was working on her math homework one afternoon, Ephram stole Madison away to the piano, and played.

As his fingers moved over the keys it was like every cell in his body came alive. It was all converging. He was playing his piece for his muse and she was sitting just inches away. Ephram poured his heart and soul into his playing, and when he was finished, he was so fit-to-burst it was all he could do to keep from throwing Madison down on the piano bench and kissing her for all he was worth.

As the final note faded away, he turned to look at her. Madison was staring at the music on the stand. She didn't move.

"What's wrong?" Ephram asked. "You hated it. You hated it, didn't you?"

Oh, God. What had he been thinking? It was so juvenile, so unpolished, so fifth grade. . . .

"No! Not at all!" Madison protested, a little too much. "It was so—"

"Bad," Ephram said, shoving the music sheets together to hide them. "Really bad. I knew it."

"Don't be crazy," Madison said, putting her hand on his arm. "It was great. I mean, you were really rolling in the middle there. Kinda Tom Waitsy, right?"

See, this is why I'm obsessed with this girl, Ephram thought.

"You got that?" he asked, moved. She got *him.*

"How could I not?" she asked.

"Oh, God. You're dying, aren't you?" Ephram said, noting her overwhelmed expression. "You're, like, embarrassed."

"It's amazing. I love it," Madison assured him. "And the band is gonna freak out over it."

Ephram's heart caught and he smiled. "You're gonna show it to the band?" he asked. Wow. Maybe she wasn't lying to make him feel better. Maybe she really *did* like it.

"Well, *obviously*," she said. "C'm'ere, you."

Then she leaned in and kissed him, breaking every rule in the Dr. Andy Brown rule book. Ephram couldn't have cared less. She liked the song. She really liked the song.

Meanwhile, Amy was off in a la-la land of her own—this one inhabited only by her and Tommy Callahan. If someone had told her last summer that she would be celebrating an anniversary with anyone who wasn't Colin Hart, she never would have believed them. But here she was, living the giddy life, making a one-month-anniversary present for Tommy. While Ephram scribbled notes during study hall, Amy pieced together a collage card for Tommy from magazine clippings and construction paper. She shopped for the perfect gifts, looking for music she knew he loved and tokens of personal jokes they had shared. It was nice doing something for someone else. It was nice to care about someone enough to be inspired.

On the day of their anniversary, Amy put the finishing touches on her homemade gift basket and drove it over to Tommy's house. She had found his address in the phone book and Mapquest-ed it out. But as she followed the directions to the outskirts of town, her heart dropped further and further. Amy wasn't just driving into the crappier part of Everwood. She was driving into the crappiest of the crappier neighborhoods: the trailer park. And as she pulled Irv's truck to a stop in front of the trailer marked "Callahan," she was filled with a mixture of guilt, sorrow, and embarrassment.

For a moment, Amy thought about turning the truck around and leaving. She didn't belong there. She knew she was going to feel like a moron carrying a huge basket full of frivolous stuff over to a trailer where spending money on frivolous stuff was probably frowned upon. But she was here. She had made this gift for Tommy. And she wanted to give it to him.

She made herself get out of the truck, crossed the street to the backdrop of a revving motorcycle engine, and, heart pounding with trepidation, knocked on the door. Amy knew less than nothing about Tommy's family. Who knew who would answer? What was she doing there?

The door opened before she could flee. A perfectly normal but tired-looking woman peeked out.

"Can I help you?"

Tommy's mother. The family resemblance was totally obvious. Oh, God. What if she didn't know about Amy?

"Oh . . . hi," Amy said. "Um . . ."

Say something! she told herself.

"Are you from the church?" Tommy's mom asked.

This is bad. This is waaaay bad, Amy thought.

"No. I think I must have the wrong place," she said, thinking quickly. "I'm sorry to bother you."

Then she turned on her heel and rushed back to her truck, feeing guiltier still and more than a little freaked out. So this was Tommy's world. She had no idea what to think.

A couple of days later Amy was staring at an F in Spanish class. A big fat F right on top of her homework paper. Could this week possibly get any worse?

"Señor Brown," Mr. Walker said, handing back

the assignment. *"Necesitas estudiar mas. Mucho mas."*

Amy glanced at Ephram sympathetically. She wasn't the only one who needed to study more, apparently. Ephram caught her eye and lifted his paper flashing his own matching F. Amy showed him hers and he smirked.

"Whatever," she said as the bell rang. "It was a stupid assignment. Who could possibly fill four pages on the tortilla and its influence on Mayan culture?"

As she spoke, she saw Page shoving her own paper into her backpack with a smile. There was a huge A at the top of her neatly typed work. Amy rolled her eyes.

"Fortunately we'll get a second chance in summer *escuela*," Ephram joked as they gathered their things.

"No worries. This is totally fixable," Amy said confidently.

"Wow. Can you cry on command, too?" Ephram asked.

Amy smiled and led him over to the front of the room, where Señor Walker was organizing his desk.

"Look, we're really . . . ," Ephram began.

"En espanol, Señor Brown," the teacher said.

Ephram glanced at Amy, clearly ready to strangle the guy. "Uh . . . *estamos mucho* . . . uh . . . *embarazada."*

The teacher smirked and Amy cringed. "You just said we're very pregnant," she told Ephram.

"I'll let you fix this," he said, stepping aside.

"*Señor, podemos hacer . . . uh . . . credito extra, por favor?*" Amy asked. "*Quiero hacer mejor.*"

"*Bueno,*" Señor Walker said. "*Para credito extra, quiero que preperen una comida autentica.*"

Amy glanced at Ephram. He looked as clueless as she felt.

"I'm letting you do an extra-credit project," the teacher explained.

"Cool. What do we have to do? A time-line history on the piñata?" Ephram asked.

Señor Walker shot him an admonishing glance. "I would like for you both to prepare an authentic Mexican meal," he said, "for the entire class. Translate the recipes into Spanish and bring it all in by Monday."

It was all Amy could do to keep from dropping her head back in frustration.

"Perfect," she said as she followed Ephram out. "Hope you know how to cook."

"About as well as I speak Spanish," Ephram replied.

Saturday afternoon Amy met up with Ephram to do a little grocery shopping for Spanish class. She was practically skipping as she crossed Main Street, even when she saw that Bright was standing with him. Not even her obnoxious brother could bring her down just then. She had given Tommy his present the night before and he had *loved* it. Plus he'd given her an amazing gift as well: a brand-new BlackBerry. Now she could text message him every five seconds if she wanted to.

Not that she would. Maybe every ten.

"Hey," Amy said as she joined Ephram and Bright on the sidewalk.

Bright looked anywhere but at her. "Dad's birthday is tomorrow night," he said. "Mom wants you to come."

"Yeah. I was planning to," Amy said. Which she was, even though she knew it was going to be completely and totally awkward. Her dad's birthday was always a big thing. Skipping it would be like ignoring Christmas.

"Whatever. Just do us all a favor and bring a present," Bright said. Then he turned to Ephram. "I'm out."

The two guys knocked hands and Bright walked away. Amy found she felt a little less heartbroken watching him go. Was she just giddy over Tommy or was she actually getting used to being the outsider in her own family?

"Wow. I think that's the longest conversation I've had with him in two weeks. Felt good," she told Ephram.

"Ready for Nacho Fest 2004?" he joked.

Amy smiled. She'd forgotten how Ephram always managed to make her smile no matter what the situation.

"Let's go," she said, heading into the grocery store.

Amy grabbed a cart and as Ephram followed her into the first aisle she couldn't help noting the peculiarity of the moment. Grocery shopping wasn't usually something she did with her guy friends. It was kind of novel.

"I poached a menu from Taco Bell," Ephram said, pulling a wrinkled piece of paper out of his pocket. "Figured we can use it as source material."

"Works for me," Amy said, bypassing the milk and OJ.

Ephram's cell phone trilled and he smiled when he saw the caller ID.

Madison, Amy thought instantly. She recognized that smile. That private, I-can't-wait-to-talk-to-this-person smile.

"Hang on a sec," Ephram said to Amy. "Hey you," he said into the phone. "Yeah. You want me to pick you up? Cool. See you then."

He hung up the phone, all grins, and Amy smirked. "I take it things are going well with you and Madison?"

"Yeah . . . you know." He was blushing like a schoolgirl. He looked away, grabbed a bag of Tostitos, and tossed them into the cart.

"Is it too weird, us talking about this?" Amy asked, feeling very mature for acknowledging the fact that she and Ephram had a history, however indefinable it was.

"No. I don't feel weird at all," he said. "Do you?"

"No. Uh-uh," she said, even though she did feel a little weird. Of course she was sure she would have felt even stranger about it if Ephram had Madison and she didn't have Tommy. Right now, with the way things were, it was like a draw.

Oh, yeah, Amy. Very mature.

"Great. So . . . what do you want to know?" Ephram asked as they continued to the next aisle. "I mean, she's awesome. She actually likes me, which is odd."

"No, it's not," Amy said with a slight laugh. "I'm glad it worked out with you two. It must be cool to have so much in common. The whole music thing. So did she ever actually *see* the Beatles play, or . . . ?"

Ephram smiled at her joke. "Ha-ha. Funny," he said. "And how's Rico Suave? You guys sharing needles yet, or what?"

Amy rolled her eyes. "I know Bright played him to be this big crack addict, but he's not like that. He's actually really smart," she said. "I think you'd like him."

Ephram nodded, not looking all that convinced. As they turned the corner into the next aisle, Amy's BlackBerry chimed. It took her a second to respond to the new ringer in her life. When she finally fished it out of her jacket pocket, Ephram's eyes widened.

"Whoa. Is that a BlackBerry?" he asked.

Amy read the message and smiled. *PHARMACY. 4PM. BE THERE.*

"Yeah. Tommy gave it to me for our one-month anniversary," Amy said, preening a bit.

"What do you get for your one-year? A GPS tracking system?" Ephram joked. Then he grabbed a couple of packages of Velveeta and turned to her. "I'm thinking this, a couple of bags of chips, and we're in the clear. What do you say?"

Amy scoffed and pushed the cart forward. "Keep walking, amigo."

As they moved along the back of the store, Amy found herself smiling privately and realized it had been a really long time since she had felt this happy for such a sustained period. But it was fun, hanging with Ephram. And after shopping she was going to the pharmacy to meet Tommy. There might have been a lot of messed-up stuff in her life, but just then, in that moment, things were actually good.

At 4 P.M. sharp, Amy was rushing down the sidewalk to meet up with Tommy. She had already dropped the groceries at home and she was free for the rest of the night. She grinned when she saw him waiting outside for her, her lips already tingling for a kiss.

"Hey! You're never gonna believe what I did. I tried to BlackBerry you this really sappy message and I think I wound up text-messaging some Japanese businessman instead," Amy said. "Now he won't stop writing me."

She went in for the hug, but Tommy pulled away. Instantly Amy's heart plummeted. He'd never done that before.

"Everything okay?" she asked, suddenly nervous.

"I have a question for you," he said, sounding seriously defensive. His body language was all tense and closed off. "Two days ago, I'm at the pharmacy. Where were you?"

"I dunno. At school probably," she said.

"I'm talking about after school."

Oh, no. Oh nonononono, Amy thought. Did Tommy know she had stopped by his house? How could he? Surveillance cameras?

"Uh . . . I don't really remember," she said, stalling for time.

"That's funny, because my *mom* seems to remember," he said, squaring his shoulders. "She says she saw someone who looked a lot like you at my house the other day. Only you pretended to be from church."

"No," Amy said, feeling sick to her stomach. "That was a mistake."

"So you *were* there," Tommy said, raising his voice.

"Yeah, but—"

"What were you doing?!" he shouted, his eyes flashing.

Amy's heart fluttered uncertainly. He was angry. *Really* angry. And she didn't like it.

"I was gonna give you your gift," she said.

"And you didn't think maybe you should tell me about that?" he demanded.

"I decided I wanted to give it to you in person, and then—"

"You're lying to *me* now, too?" he interjected.

"No! I'm sorry! Look, I was just trying to surprise you," Amy said. *Why is this getting so out of hand?* she thought.

"You come to my house totally uninvited and then you don't bother to tell me?" he shouted. "You met my mother for God's sake, and you don't even mention it. Who does that? I mean, did I ask you to come by? Did I *say* that would be okay?"

Amy blinked, totally confused. "No . . . but—"

"No. Then that's it," he blurted out. "Either you're invited to someone's house or you're not. And you weren't. So in the future, if I don't ask you to do something, don't do it. Period."

Amy felt as if she was watching a total breakdown. This wasn't Tommy—not the Tommy she knew. He wasn't making any sense and he was being really loud and scary about it.

"Excuse me?" she said. "Are you mad that I came to your house, or that I didn't tell you about it?"

Tommy paused, looking snagged. "Look, just don't do it again, okay?" he said. "I gotta get back to work."

Then he turned and disappeared into the pharmacy, leaving Amy on the street to wonder what on Earth had just happened.

That night Ephram pulled his car up to the garage where Madison's band practiced and got out, slamming the door. It was amazing that just a few weeks ago he had been totally nervous coming here, not knowing where he stood or if Madison even knew he existed. Now it was old hat. He was the boyfriend. The boyfriend coming to pick up the gorgeous lead singer of the band.

Ephram was a badass. And he didn't even flinch when he saw Jay opening the door of his hot, red sports car.

"She's in there, going over the latest," Jay told him.

Ephram's face lit up. The latest? That must have been *his* song. The band was working on his song!

"Cool, so it's coming together good then?" Ephram asked, feeling beyond cool that he could chat with Jay about *his* music. "How's that last progression after the chorus? I was thinking about tweaking it, but—"

"Dude, what're you talking about?" Jay asked.

"The song that I . . ."

Jay smirked, and Ephram realized Madison and the band were not working on his song. From the look on his face, Jay knew nothing *about* his song.

"Never mind," Ephram said quickly.

But it was too late. Jay had figured it out.

"No, it's cool," he said, amused. "I wrote lots of songs for chicks when I was your age. It's totally normal, prepubescent behavior. Just tell me it's not called 'Madison.'"

Wow. I am a totally predictable loser, Ephram thought, his face burning with embarrassment.

Jay laughed, rubbing in the misery, and Ephram looked at the ground. How many humiliating moments could one person take before he spontaneously combusted?

"Don't stress, kid," Jay said. "If the song's good, it's good." Then he paused. "Is it good?"

"Obviously not. Otherwise you would've heard it by now," Ephram snapped.

"True that," Jay said, tilting his head in mock sympathy. "Sucks to be you."

He got in his car, his words ringing in Ephram's ears. Jay had absolutely no idea how very right he was. Ephram turned and stalked into the garage, totally ready to pick a fight.

"Ephram!" Madison said with a huge grin. "Perfect timing. We were just wrapping up."

She leaned in for a kiss, but Ephram pulled away. His hands were jammed so hard into his pockets he was certain he was going to rip right through them.

"You should've told me the truth," he said. "I could've handled it."

Madison's face fell slightly. "What are you talking about?"

"Instead I come all the way over here and wind up looking like an idiot in front of your ex-boyfriend, which is hard to do considering he's got the IQ of a potato," Ephram rambled.

"Slow down," Madison said. "I have no idea—"

"The song!" Ephram blurted out. "You never showed them the song. You never planned on showing them the song. Instead you lied to me about it. Why?"

Madison fell back from him and bit her lip. "I don't know."

"That's great," Ephram spat. "That's really helpful."

"I'm sorry. I never should have said I would show the song to the band, because you're right. I wasn't going to," she said.

Okay. Not exactly the apology and explanation Ephram was looking for. His song must have blown serious chunks.

"So you hate it," he said, feeling awful.

"No. I'm just not comfortable sharing that kind of stuff," Madison said. "Especially here."

"Because of Jay?" Ephram asked.

"Because of everyone," Madison replied. "Because . . . it's a little embarrassing."

Ephram wanted to hurl. She was ashamed of him. Embarrassed by him. And to think that five minutes ago he was all psyched to see her. And this afternoon? Telling Amy how much Madison liked him? How totally gullible could he be?

"Ugh. This is coming out all wrong," Madison said.

Ephram had to get out of there, stat.

"No. I get it. It's embarrassing. I embarrassed you. I better go before I do it again."

"It's not you, Ephram," Madison said as he backed away. "Can we just talk about this?"

"It's no big deal. Forget it," Ephram said. "I'll catch you later."

Then he got the heck out of there before he could embarrass either one of them further.

Ephram was making Amy totally tense. He kept looking at his cell phone like he was waiting for it to explode. And he kept pacing, like he couldn't sit still for five seconds. It was making her want to hurl the vegetables she was chopping at his head.

"Why is there no reception anywhere in this

house?" Ephram said tersely. "I'm getting, like, one bar."

He paced behind her and aimed the phone at the window—*like that's going to help,* Amy thought as she chopped the vegetables a little more vigorously. As if she wasn't clenched enough already, she had to deal with Alexander Graham Bell freaking out.

"Are you gonna help or are you going to obsess over your phone all day?" she asked, bringing the knife down repeatedly on an unsuspecting mushroom. "My dad's birthday dinner is in an hour. I'd like to get there on time, thanks."

"I am helping," Ephram said. "And I'm not obsessing."

"Look, I don't know what you're freaking out over. She's probably just got other things going on," Amy said.

Like Tommy does. Which is exactly why he hasn't called me to apologize for losing it on me yesterday.

"Like what?" Ephram asked, sounding almost hopeful to hear a plausible answer.

Amy felt as if she was going to burst out of her skin from irritation. Why was he asking her this? Couldn't he just chill out for five seconds? Couldn't he see that he was just making her more tense?

"I don't know, maybe she's having a *jam session,*" she said sarcastically. "Or a Bingo night. Whatever it is, I'm pretty sure she's not sitting around wondering when she should call her high school boyfriend."

"Uh-oh. Sounds like someone had a fight with Tommy Crackhead," Ephram shot back.

"Like you could even tell anymore if I was upset about something," Amy said, whirling on him.

"You're right. I probably couldn't," he replied.

"I guess you can only be friends with one Abbott at a time, is that it?" Amy demanded, still chopping. "Bright's the lucky winner. But hey, maybe next year you'll be my friend again. Kind of a trade-off system?"

"You know, I don't see you making time for me," Ephram said. "As usual, Amy gets a boyfriend and everyone else in the universe ceases to exist. I guess I can't take it too personally, since you don't even speak to blood relatives anymore."

All right, that was it. Where the heck did he get off? Amy dropped the knife and turned to Ephram.

"How would you know?" she demanded. "You haven't asked me about it. We're standing in my grandparents' kitchen right now and you didn't even say one word."

"What do you want me to say?" Ephram asked, throwing out his hands. "That I think you're completely wacked? 'Cause I do! You moved out of your house over some guy you barely know—"

"You think this is about Tommy? You think he's

the reason my life is where it is right now?" Amy asked.

"I don't know—"

"That's right, you don't know!" Amy blurted, feeling a diatribe coming on. "I've been on antidepressants for the last few months. Did you know that? Did you know that I didn't actually ask to move out of my house? That my parents basically *kicked* me out? My dad can't look me in the eyes anymore. My grandparents are only tolerating me because they feel guilty. So, first I lost Colin, then I lost my family."

Okay, she was getting pretty deep into pity territory. It wasn't like Amy wanted Ephram to feel sorry for her. She just wanted him to get it—get that he had missed a lot when he'd suddenly stopped bothering to talk to her.

"But you know what? It's fine. Because I met this guy a few weeks ago who made it all better. Yeah. That's what happened."

There was a moment of complete silence and Amy went back to chopping. She felt a little better after getting all that off her chest, but not much.

"Look, this all went down pretty recently, and you never came to me," Ephram said.

"No. You never came to me," she replied.

Suddenly the oven started to smoke and Amy jumped for the oven mitts. She opened the door to find a nice big tray of blackened enchiladas.

"Great," she said, pulling it out.

"I'm out of here," Ephram said. He grabbed his coat and stalked out. "You have a visitor!" he shouted from outside.

Amy dropped the tray of smoking food on the counter and glanced out the window. Her heart stopped when she saw Tommy there. She pulled on her jacket and walked out, not sure what to expect.

"I come in peace," Tommy said, holding out a single red rose.

Part of Amy wanted to take it, but she resisted. She was still mad.

"I think we need to talk about what happened yesterday," she said.

"Yeah, yeah. I know," Tommy said. "I'm really sorry."

"Look, I don't know where that came from, but if we're going to be together, then I need to understand what's going on with you."

Tommy blinked. Clearly he thought this was going to be easier. "I said I was sorry. . . ."

"I don't want an apology," Amy said. "I want an explanation."

"Can't we just pretend like the whole thing never happened?" he asked.

"No. We can't do that. I'm sorry," Amy replied.

She felt a bit proud of herself for standing up to him. And at the same time her heart was slamming around painfully.

"I was embarrassed, okay?" Tommy said, sounding like he was hoping that was all he would have to say. He looked at Amy and she stared right back. She still hadn't heard an explanation.

"Have you ever been called white trash?" he said finally. "Or had to stand in line at a grocery store to pay for stuff with food stamps?"

Amy had to glance away. She knew things were bad for Tommy and his family, but she had no idea they were *that* bad.

"It's about as humiliating as it sounds," he said. "Your dad is a doctor. Your mom's the friggin' mayor of Everwood. My mom . . . she cleans motels for six bucks an hour. My job at the pharmacy isn't some after-school, saving-up-for-a-car kind of job, you know? What I make goes to rent, water, and electricity."

Amy looked down, starting to regret taking a stand. It clearly pained Tommy to talk about this stuff and she was the one who had dragged it out of him.

"We used to have this great old house up on Mulberry, but when my parents split, he kept the house. But he didn't keep us," Tommy continued. "All my mom could afford was three hundred bucks a month for a two-bedroom trailer. I lost most of my friends. It's a tough sell, you know? Getting kids to come hang at the trailer park." He took a deep breath and let it out loudly. "Anyways, I guess I didn't want you to see where I lived and that part of my life, because I was afraid I'd lose you, too."

The guilt Amy had felt when she had dropped by his house came rushing back. "And then I proved you right by freaking out and leaving."

"Yeah, well. You were sweet enough to lie about it," Tommy said, looking at the ground.

"I'm sorry I did that," Amy said.

"It's okay. I probably would've done the same thing," Tommy said. "It's weird, isn't it?"

"Not that weird. I mean, so you live in a trailer park. So what? I'm living in the guest room of my grandparents' house. It's just where we live. It's not who we are or the reason we're together."

Amy bent at the knee and tilted her head, attempting to get into Tommy's line of sight.

"I'm not going anywhere," she said with a smile.

Tommy finally looked up and offered the rose again, cracking a smile himself. "Could I take you out to dinner?" he asked. "I know this really great restaurant I think I can get us into. You know, burgers . . . fries . . . McNuggets."

Amy smiled, took the rose and Tommy's arm, and headed toward the sidewalk, forgetting all about her fight with Ephram, all about the burned enchiladas on the counter, and all about anything else she was supposed to be doing that night.

Tommy made it all too easy to forget about everything.

Ephram came home from his altercation with Amy and slammed the door. He stalked into the dining room to find his father setting the table. Ephram tossed his jacket over the back of a chair.

"What's for dinner?"

"What are you doing here?" his father asked, surprised and maybe even a bit annoyed.

What the heck? Just the other day his father had been lecturing him about spending more time at home, hanging out with Delia more often. He'd been all upset that Ephram was forgoing the rest of his life to be with Madison 24/7. Now he was here and he was getting confused and irritated looks? Ephram could not win.

"This is where I come at the end of the day. It's where I live. It's where I sleep," Ephram said. Then he noticed that the good plates were out and there were candles lit around the centerpiece. "What's with the table?"

"Linda's coming over for dinner," his father said. "She should be here any minute."

"Cool. Maybe I'll take Delia over to Sal's for some pizza and video games," Ephram said as his father handed him his jacket back, removing it from the vicinity of his perfectly set table.

"Delia's at Brittany's," his father said.

Ephram stopped in his tracks. Here he thought he was going to get some bonding time with the little sis—maybe one good side of this whole fight with Madison—and she wasn't even around. What was he going to do all night? Sit up in his room and wallow?

"I figured you'd be with Madison tonight," his father said, making Ephram feel even worse. "Wait. Why aren't you with Madison tonight?"

"Would you believe that we decided our relationship was strong enough that we don't have to spend every waking moment together?" Ephram asked.

"No," his father said.

"Then I think we're in a fight."

The doorbell rang and his father looked from the door to Ephram, clearly torn.

"What happened?" his dad asked.

"I don't know. I wrote her this song. She didn't like it. I got mad. And now she's not calling me."

The doorbell rang again and both Ephram and his dad looked toward the door for the second time.

"It's hard, isn't it?" Ephram asked.

"What?"

"Trying to have a relationship and a life at the same time," Ephram said.

His father looked at him, realizing that he had basically scolded Ephram for not being able to do both.

"Yes, but I want to talk to you about this," he said. "I'll tell Linda that we have to postpone dinner. Then you can tell me everything that happened."

Yeah. That sounds like fun, Ephram thought. "It's okay. That's pretty much it," he said.

"Well, you're welcome to join us," his father said.

"I'm fairly certain that seeing you in date mode would scar me for the rest of my life," Ephram said. "I'll be in my room."

Ephram started upstairs for that night of wallowing. After the couple of days he'd had, he was starting to realize that maybe his father had been right to lecture him about balancing life and a relationship—a tad hypocritical and self-righteous, but right. He was fighting with Amy, he felt as if he hadn't seen Delia in days, and his schoolbooks were pretty much gathering dust at this point. Maybe it was about time he started being more conscious of staying true to himself while still being true to Madison.

If Madison was even his to be true to anymore.

Amy was brushing her hair out before bed, smiling to herself over the perfect evening she had shared with Tommy. Feeding each other McNuggets, smooching over milk shakes. . . . If anyone else told her *they* had done these things she'd think they were far too sappy and gross. But she was loving every minute of it.

"Where were you tonight?" Her grandmother's voice burst into her reverie.

Amy turned to find her standing in the doorway of the guest room.

"I was out with Tommy. Why?" she asked. Then the sour, disappointed expression on her grandmother's face brought it home. She had missed her father's birthday.

"Oh my God," Amy said, everything inside of her twisting into knots. "I totally forgot. Is it too late? Can I—"

"They've all gone to bed," her grandmother said, arms crossed over her chest. "I know you're having a tough time, and it's not like I agree with everything your folks are doing, but to miss your father's birthday—"

"I know. I know. I screwed up," Amy said, her mind reeling. "I really meant to—"

"No one cares what you *meant* to do. The only thing anyone's going to remember is that you weren't there," her grandmother said sternly. "There was one person your dad wanted to see tonight: *You*."

Okay. Rub it in a little there, Grandma, Amy thought. But she knew her grandmother was right. She had to fix this. There had to be a way. Unfortunately nothing was coming to mind.

"So what do I do?"

"I don't know. From the look on your dad's face I'd say it'd take a helluva birthday present," she replied. "Hope you saved your allowance. Night, Amy."

Her grandmother walked out and Amy was left

feeling all hollow and helpless. She couldn't believe she had forgotten about her father's birthday. And for what? For McDonald's? What was *wrong* with her?

Maybe sometimes the fact that being with Tommy made her forget everything else was great, but other times . . .

Other times, it was the worst possible thing.

Tommy was amazing, but was he really worth all of this? Was he really worth fighting with Ephram and not talking to Bright and not living at home and making her father feel about a hundred times worse than she did right then? Was he really worth all the loss?

CHAPTER 10

Whether Tommy was good for Amy or bad for her, at moments like this, was totally irrelevant. They were up at the Point, the overlook where all the kids in town went to make out in their parents' cars, and they were doing just that. And Amy was loving every minute of it. Tommy was an amazing kisser. He was sweet and gentle and perfect and tender and—

Wait a minute. Was he trying to unbutton her jeans?

"Oh, whoa!" Amy said, pulling away. Then she instantly felt like a big baby.

"What? What'd I do?" Tommy asked, his lips all puffy from kissing.

"Nothing. I just . . . that was new," Amy said, pushing her hair behind her ears.

"I'm sorry. Oh, God. Did I . . . did I just freak

you out?" Tommy asked, sliding a couple of inches away.

"No. Please don't apologize. I just need to regroup here for a second," Amy said. "I'm not really used to . . . that."

"Really? You mean you never—"

"No . . . no. Did you think I had?" Amy asked, surprised.

"Well . . . yeah. I guess you always just seem so comfortable and together with yourself. I just assumed you and Colin had already—"

"No," Amy said. "We never did." She took a deep breath and smiled. "But that's a really nice compliment considering that's not at all how I feel."

"Coulda fooled me," Tommy said, and Amy's smile widened.

For a second there they had been in the awkward danger zone, but this was better. This was actually kind of nice, this . . . honesty.

"I hope you know I would have never done that if I knew—"

"I know," Amy said. She reached out and took his hand, playing with his fingers. "And I'm not gonna be this way forever."

"When you're ready, I'm ready," Tommy said, looking her in the eye. "And if you're never ready, that's cool with me. I don't care. It's not why I'm into you, Amy."

Her heart warmed and her grip on his hand tightened slightly. "It's my winning personality, isn't it?" she joked.

"Well, that and the free Skittles," he said, moving in to kiss her again.

As Amy touched her lips to his and felt his hands in her hair, she felt entirely safe. No pressure, no awkwardness. Just Tommy. And she trusted him completely.

"Well? Do you *want* to?" Laynie asked on Monday after school.

Amy blushed and shrugged. She and Laynie were sitting on the bed in the guest room, books open and totally ignored. Amy had just related the tale of Saturday night and Laynie couldn't have been more intrigued.

"I didn't *not* want to," Amy said, leaning back against the headboard. "I just didn't even think it was a possibility. In my mind it was never on the menu, you know?"

She took a sip of her tea and looked at Laynie for a reaction.

"And now it is," she said with a sly smile.

"Yeah," Amy said, recalling how very possible it had felt. "Big time."

"So go for it," Laynie said, whacking her knee. "Why not? He's great. You like him, right?"

"Yeah. I like him a lot," Amy said, feeling that

tickling sensation of giddiness she felt every time she thought about Tommy.

"And he probably knows what he's doing," Laynie said.

"Laynie!" Amy cracked an embarrassed smile and put her tea down on the bedside table. "But just out of curiosity, what is it, exactly, that I'm supposed to do?"

"You don't have to worry about that part," Laynie said, all wise. "You can just sorta lie there at first."

"Gee, when you put it that way, it sounds so romantic," Amy said.

"That's just it—it's not gonna be romantic," Laynie told her, causing a pang of disappointment in Amy's heart. "I mean, it could be, and maybe it will be, but if you build it up in your mind as this big thing that's gonna change your life forever, you'll just wind up disappointed. Trust me. The lower your expectations are, the better."

Nice, Amy thought. *Sounds about as fun as a trip to the dentist.*

"Maybe I'm not ready to do this after all," she said, hating the sound of the words. Just when she'd talked herself into it . . .

"That's fine," Laynie said. "Just don't wait too long or you'll wind up like Rachel Hofer's sister."

Amy blinked. "What happened to Rachel Hofer's sister?"

"Twenty-nine years old. Never did it," Laynie said. "Now she's petrified that she's gonna die a virgin. It's really sad."

"God," Amy said. She definitely didn't want to be *that* girl. Maybe it was time to stop taking all this so seriously. Time to just get out there and get it over with. It was never going to be perfect, after all, because it was never going to be with Colin. So why not just find out what all the fuss was about? Because one thing was for certain—Amy did not want to die a virgin.

Later that evening, Amy was starting to think that dying a virgin didn't seem like a half-bad idea. If it meant she could avoid doing what she was about to do, then it was definitely a viable option. She stood outside Dr. Brown's office on the cold sidewalk, the wind blowing her ponytail all over the place, trying to make her feet move.

Just do it, she told herself. *You have no other choice and you're not the kind of idiot who's going to go into this unprepared.*

This thought was somehow enough to make her open the door and step inside. Dr. Brown was in the waiting area, turning off lights. He looked shocked to see her. Not that she could blame him. If anyone had told her she would have ever willingly talked to Andrew Brown again, she would have laughed until she cried.

"Amy," he said finally. "I'm sorry, but your grand-mother's already gone for the day."

"I know," she said. But then she found she couldn't say anything else. She wasn't supposed to be there. After Dr. Brown had basically decided to let Colin die on the operating table, she had promised herself she would never speak to him again. It just made her reason for dealing with him ironic. Seriously, deadly ironic.

"Are you okay?" he asked.

"Do you have a minute?" Amy said, trying to eradicate the picture of Colin from her mind. "I need to talk to you about something."

"Sure. Come on in," Dr. Brown said, looking thoroughly confused.

Amy followed him into his office and shut the door behind her. He sat down at his desk and looked at the chair in front of him as if suggesting she sit. Amy found she wasn't quite ready for that level of comfort, so she stood. Close enough to the door for a hasty escape if one were needed.

"Look, I know this is weird. And believe me, if there was anyone else in this entire town I could go to, I would," she began. "But since there isn't, I was hoping we could just pretend that we were . . . fine."

"I can do that," he said.

Amy took a deep breath, pulling together every last scrap of courage she had in her little body. Then, she blurted it out.

"I need to go on the pill."

The words just hung in the room for a second, giving them even more weight than they naturally carried.

Say something, Amy willed him. *Say anything.* Unfortunately, Dr. Brown was looking like he'd rather be anywhere but here. *Join the club.*

"Birth control?" he said.

"Yeah. So what do I need to do?" Amy said, desperate to get this over with as quickly as possible. "Blood test, or—"

"Let's . . . slow down for a second and let me catch up here," he said. "Are you currently involved in a sexual relationship?"

"Um . . . what do you mean, exactly?" Amy asked. "I mean, I'm in a relationship, but we haven't had . . . it hasn't happened."

Dr. Brown looked seriously relieved. What was his deal? He was acting like he was her father or something.

"Oh. Okay, well, this is good," he said. "So this is simply a precautionary measure."

"Yeah."

"And you're just thinking about having sex."

"Obviously, or I wouldn't be here," Amy said curtly. "Look, if this is too weird for you because of the whole family connection and you being my aunt's boyfriend—"

"I'm a doctor," he said. "Doctors don't get weird."

"Because Laynie told me about a Planned Parenthood in Denver that I could go to, but I was hoping I wouldn't have to go—"

"You don't have to. I'm happy to help," he said. "I just want to make sure that you've thought this decision through carefully."

Amy finally realized that she wasn't going to be getting out of the office quite as quickly as she had hoped. She walked around the chair and sat down, letting out a sigh.

"Well, I looked up all the possibilities on the net, Norplant and all that," she said. "But the pill seemed like the right choice," she told him, feeling all thorough and wise.

"I was talking about the decision to have sex," he said, making her squirm. "Have you talked to anyone about it? Anyone other than Laynie?"

"Who would I talk to?" Amy asked defensively.

"I know you're having a difficult time with your family right now, but I'm sure your father would want to help you—"

Adults could be so dumb. "No offense, Dr. Brown, but even if I wasn't in a massive fight with my dad right now, I still wouldn't talk to him about it. Or my mom. I think these things are private."

"What about your grandmother? There's a lot of compassion under all that khaki."

Amy sighed again. "I came here specifically when I knew she wouldn't be here. Does that answer your question?" He looked so disappointed it would have been heartbreaking if she didn't detest him so much. "Look, I'm sixteen. I'm thinking about having sex and I want to be safe if and when I decide to do it. Is that so wrong?"

"No. No it's not," he replied. "You realize that the pill doesn't protect against any STDs. . . ."

"I know. I have condoms," Amy said.

The poor guy looked sick to his stomach. "Look, Amy, I'm sure I'm the last person you want advice from right now, but I'm gonna give you a little," he said. "Don't be afraid to wait until everything is right. You're never gonna get this moment back."

Amy felt a squirming uneasiness in her chest. "Well, I appreciate what you're saying, Dr. Brown, but I *had* the right person in my life. Unfortunately we ran out of time. I'm just being realistic."

She looked him in the eye and was gratified to see the sorrow and regret reflected there.

"So will you write the prescription?"

"I'll have to take a medical history, get blood and urine samples and . . . if it all checks out, yes, I'll write the prescription."

Amy didn't feel as relieved as she thought she would, but at least it was done. She was going to have sex and she was going to be responsible about it. Everything was going to be just fine.

• • •

"What are you doing Saturday night?" Tommy asked Amy over slices at Sal's Pizza.

Amy took a sip of her water. "I think I'm going out to dinner with Orlando Bloom," she answered. "No wait. That's Friday. . . ."

Tommy kicked her ankle lightly under the table and Amy smiled. "Just kidding. Why? What's up?"

"Chris Bradley's having a party at his parents' ski chalet," Tommy said. "It's totally beautiful out there and it's gonna be pretty huge. Thought it might be fun."

"Sure. Sounds great," Amy said. Then, with a thrill of excitement, she realized exactly *how* great. "Actually, it sounds kind of perfect."

"Perfect how?" Tommy asked.

"It's just . . . a ski chalet, all snowy and fancy," she said, flushing. "Sounds like it could be kind of romantic, doesn't it?"

Tommy narrowed his eyes. He had yet to catch on. "I guess. Yeah."

"So maybe it would be a perfect place to . . . you know . . ."

Realization dawned on Tommy's face, but he just looked confused, not psyched. "Seriously?"

"Why not?" Amy said, barreling ahead. "It's better than doing it at the Point, isn't it?"

"Yeah, it is . . . I just, I mean . . ."

He ran his hand over his hair and shifted in his

seat a little. "When did this happen?" he asked
finally.

"I've just been thinking about it and I think I'm
ready to take the next step," Amy said. "And stop
looking so shocked, 'cause it's freaking me out."

"I'm sorry, I'm just taken aback here," Tommy
said. "I mean, the other night—"

"Took me by surprise," Amy interjected. "But
after careful consideration and visiting a doctor—"

"You went to a doctor?" Tommy blurted.

"Well, yeah," Amy said. "I mean, if we're gonna
do this thing, I wanna be prepared."

Tommy brought his hand to the side of his head,
elbow on the table, and looked at her, totally per-
plexed.

"I thought you'd be happy," Amy said, her confidence waning.

"I am. I'm totally happy," Tommy replied. "I
just . . . I don't want you to be doing this for any
reason other than the fact that you want to."

"I do want to," Amy said. Then, because he was
being so sweet and honest with her, she decided to
be perfectly honest right back. "Would it make you
feel horrible if I told you that part of me just kind
of wants to get it over with?" she asked.

Tommy blinked. "Well, it wouldn't make me feel
great, you know?"

"See, none of this is happening the way I thought
it would," she said. "For as long as I can remember,

I thought it would be with Colin." She looked at him and he swallowed, taking this in. She could tell her words had stung. "I'm sorry if I hurt your feelings."

Tommy sighed. "No. *I'm* sorry," he said. "I totally missed it before. And you're awesome."

Amy smiled slightly. "Anyway, we don't have to do this if you don't want to. . . ."

Tommy smiled in his lopsided way and reached across the table for her hand.

"What time should I pick you up on Saturday?"

Amy looked at him and grinned uncontrollably. This was good. This was right. Or as right as it was going to be. It was really going to happen.

Amy sat with Tommy on a small love seat at the packed-to-the-rafters ski chalet party, trying to pay attention to what he was saying. Unfortunately it totally wasn't working. They both knew what they were there for. All Amy could think about was when, where, and how soon it was going to happen. Did Tommy know of a room to go to? Was he waiting for her to make the first move? Why didn't he just take her hand and lead her upstairs already?

"Amy!" Laynie called out, walking over to the couch. "Can I talk to you for a second? I think I lost my ring."

"What ring?" Amy asked.

"It's my mom's. It's real," Laynie said. "Could you just . . . ? Two seconds."

Amy glanced apologetically at Tommy.

"It's cool. I'll meet you upstairs?" he said.

A sizzle of excitement shot through Amy. Yes! Upstairs was good. Unfortunately the sizzle was followed by a nervous queasiness. But that was to be expected.

"Okay," she said. "Just two seconds."

Tommy got up and headed for the stairs. Amy headed for Laynie.

"What ring are you—"

"Don't sleep with him," Laynie blurted out.

Amy blinked. Wasn't this gung ho sex girl?

"What?" she asked.

"Just trust me on this one," Laynie said, her brown eyes wide. "Don't do it."

"Look, I don't know what this is about, but Tommy's waiting for me, so . . ."

Amy started to move away, but Laynie grabbed her arm. "I don't think he's being completely honest with you," she said. "I mean . . . I *know* he's not. I think he's still dealing."

Amy rolled her eyes. "First of all, Tommy never dealt. That was just a rumor," she said. "And second of all—"

"I saw him. He was in the bathroom with a group of people—"

"This is so stupid," Amy said.

"And he was handing out baggies with these little white pills in them and people were giving him cash back," Laynie said firmly. "I don't know what you call it, but in my world, that's dealing. I'm sorry."

Amy felt like her knees were about to collapse under her. Something inside her chest withered and died. Laynie couldn't be right. Tommy couldn't be lying to her. She trusted him. They trusted each other.

"You must have seen it wrong," Amy said without much conviction. "Maybe he was in the room, but . . . that can't be right."

"If you don't believe me, then just ask him," Laynie said.

"No! I'm not gonna ask him," Amy said. The very idea sounded totally absurd. *Tommy, before we have sex, let me ask you . . . are you dealing drugs?*

"Look, I wish I hadn't seen it," Laynie said. "But actually, maybe I'm glad I did. I don't know. I just don't think you should do anything you're gonna regret. You don't want your first time to be with somebody who—"

"Somebody who what?" Amy asked.

"Somebody who you can't trust," Laynie finished.

The words were like a death knell to Amy. Then, from somewhere up above, Tommy called her name.

"Amy! You've gotta see the view from the master

bedroom," he shouted, leaning over the railing at the top of the stairs. He looked perfectly happy and totally psyched. "It's incredible."

Amy looked at Laynie, who simply shrugged. Laynie wouldn't lie to her. Not about something like this. There was just no way. And how could someone *see* something like that wrong? Hear wrong, maybe, but not see. This night had just gone from exciting to depressing in two-point-five seconds.

"Coming," Amy called out.

And as she got up and left Laynie behind, she knew what she had to do. She wove through the crowd of loud, raucous partiers and found her way to the stairs on shaky legs. At the top, Tommy took her hand and led her around the corner. Amy's palms were sweating and cold. His were completely dry. Her heart pounded as he led her into a massive oak-paneled bedroom with a huge bed and windows on every wall. The view was, in fact, intense. A huge mountain loomed in the distance, its snow cap gleaming in the moonlight.

God, this would have been perfect, Amy thought. *It would have been totally perfect.*

"It is pretty," Amy said, stalling for time.

"That's what I was just thinking," Tommy said, slipping in front of her with a smile.

He tucked both hands under her hair and cupped the back of her head, a gesture she normally relished, and kissed her on the lips. For a moment

Amy kissed him back, thinking maybe she should still just do this, but as he moved her toward the bed, her head refused. This couldn't happen, not with all the questions jamming up her brain.

She fell back into a seated position on the bed, and pulled back from him.

"Wait," she said.

"Okay," he replied instantly, ever the gentleman. "Are you having second thoughts?" he asked.

"No . . . uh . . . ," Amy said, sliding back on the bed a little. Tommy crouched in front of her. "I have to ask you something."

"Sure. You can ask me anything. You know that," he said.

"Laynie said she saw you earlier. In the bathroom?" Amy said, watching his face. No reaction. "With . . . a bunch of people."

"Yeah," Tommy said.

"She said you were dealing," Amy said, her heart thumping extra hard. There. It was out there.

Tommy sighed and dropped his head. He stood up straight and ran his hand over his brow. "If I tell you it's not what you think, you're not gonna believe me anyway, so—"

"Try me," Amy said, sitting up straight.

"Look, there's a reason that I know these guys. It's not like I'm part of their inner circle or anything. Bradley knew that I'd know a guy who could hook them up. I'm not even the point person on this."

Amy squirmed farther away from him, unable to even look at him just then. It sounded a lot like he was making excuses, like he was grasping for the right thing to say. This was insane. She thought he had never dealt. What was happening here?

"It all sounds bad, I know. I know," Tommy said, practically begging. "The worst part is, when he first asked me, I told him to forget it."

"What changed your mind?" Amy asked flatly.

"A couple of things," Tommy said. "First of all, you have to understand, this guy offered me a lot of cash just to make the connection, more than I get at the pharmacy in a month. That's, like, rent for my entire family, okay?"

Amy hated this argument. She felt badly for him that his family was in such a bad situation, but it didn't give him an excuse to deal drugs.

"And then you and I talked about coming here, and what it would mean . . . ," he added, causing a small but painful tear in her heart. "I knew that if I didn't supply the stuff, they'd never let me in."

"It didn't have to happen here," Amy said, refusing to let him use her as part of his reasoning. "You could have told me. I would have understood."

"I know, I know. I know that now," Tommy said. "I didn't want you thinking of me like this. I don't want you thinking of me as the guy people call when they need, you know . . . whatever. It's not a reputation I want to have, but I have it. I guess I was just trying to keep that from you for as long as possible."

Amy stared at him. Why couldn't there have been a better explanation than this, one that didn't make her feel so dead and awful inside? This was supposed to be an amazing, life-altering night. And now it was just . . . awful.

"But I promise you, okay. I will never, ever do anything this stupid again, okay?" Tommy said, his eyes pleading. "I swear, Amy."

Amy studied him. It seemed like he was being sincere, but who was to tell? She had thought he was being honest with her before this and he wasn't.

"Maybe we should just go," he said.

"Yeah," Amy said, all her senses dulled. Even her voice sounded fuzzy to her. "I think so."

"I'll go find our coats," Tommy said, leaving the room quickly—almost like he was relieved.

Amy, for her part, was actually relieved to see him go. She didn't want to be around him at the moment—didn't even know how she was going to last the whole trip back to town. As much as she wanted to believe he was some kind of innocent pawn, as much as she wanted to believe he was telling the truth when he said he would never do something like this again, she just couldn't. Not yet. The trust was gone. And she had a feeling nothing was ever going to be the same between her and Tommy again.

CHAPTER 11

Sometimes Ephram still couldn't believe that he had a girlfriend. He was in the boyfriend zone. But moments like these, when he was hanging out at Madison's house, studying with her on the couch with their legs entwined, it hit him: He was in a relationship. With Madison. He was a very lucky man.

And then Madison's uptight roommate, Carrie, appeared in the doorway of the living room, and all sense of euphoria fled. Carrie was so tense she made Ephram tense just by being in the same general space. Her blond hair was fanned out above her shoulders in that jagged, feathery way that was so popular, but it just made her appear even more wired.

"Did your underage boyfriend finish my Fudgsicles?" she asked Madison haughtily. She didn't even look at Ephram.

"I took *one*," he said.

"Does he not understand the concept of labels?" Carrie asked, ignoring Ephram. "The Post-it clearly said 'Carrie.'"

Madison stopped highlighting her textbook and sighed. "Why don't you ask him directly, as he's sitting right next to me?"

Ephram tried not to laugh. Madison's particular brand of sarcasm was one of his favorite things about her.

"He touches another one of my fudgy pops, I'm calling child services," Carrie said. Then she spun on her heel and stalked out of the room.

Ephram shook his head. "I can't believe I was once mad at you for not letting me meet your friends," he said.

"She's not my friend; she's my roommate," Madison replied.

"Are you stuck with her for all of college or can you switch roommates, like majors?" Ephram joked.

"The good news is she's going to visit her boyfriend in Boise this weekend," Madison said, pushing herself up a little straighter on the couch. "Which means he's either fictional or crazy."

Ephram laughed.

"But who cares? I'm just happy that we get the place to ourselves for once," Madison added.

Ephram's heart skipped a beat. He had to have heard that one wrong. She wasn't actually saying that—

"We?" he said, his voice almost cracking.

"Well, yeah, if you want to come over," Madison said, highlighting another line in her book. "It'd be nice to hang out without someone walking in on us every five minutes."

"Yeah," Ephram said, his mind reeling with the possibilities of what she might be suggesting—what they *could* do if they weren't being interrupted every five minutes. Damn it was great dating an older woman. She was just sitting there acting like it was no big deal, acting like she hadn't just propositioned him.

"She leaves around five. You can come over right after," Madison said, continuing her work as Ephram's pulse pounded in his ears. "Hopefully I'll have my paper done by then."

Trying to play it as cool as she was, Ephram returned his attention to his chemistry book. But his hands were sweating, his eyes refused to stay on the page, and his brain was not focused on chemical reactions.

He was going to have sex. With Madison. Ephram and Madison were going to have sex. And he hadn't even had to bring it up or have an awkward talk or anything. It was *her* idea. Entirely hers.

He really was a lucky, *lucky* man.

• • •

Okay, but he couldn't possibly be *that* lucky. By the next day Ephram had all but convinced himself that he was totally wrong about the whole thing. She couldn't have been propositioning him. Who would ever want to have sex with him—Ephram— king of the awkward dork-boys? And this was Madison he was talking about. She could have any guy she wanted. There was no way she would make it this easy for him.

But she *had* said that thing about not being interrupted every five minutes. And that thing about having the whole place to themselves. Those sounded like clear indicators. . . .

By the end of the school day Ephram had pretty much driven himself crazy going back and forth on the matter, so he did the only thing he could do. He consulted Bright.

"That's awesome!" was his friend's immediate reaction to the story. They were walking down Main Street on a perfectly sunny day and Ephram felt buoyed by the fact that Bright seemed so stoked.

"All she said was 'My roommate is going to Boise for the weekend,'" he reiterated, following Bright across the street.

"I know! That's awesome!" Bright repeated, unfazed by Ephram's dubious tone. "Your girl-friend just told you that you guys have her whole place to yourselves for the whole weekend. That's a serious invitation to the big leagues."

Ephram was still unconvinced. "No. No. We haven't even *talked* about sex yet," he said. This was one of the arguments he'd been having with himself all day, so he figured he'd bounce it off Bright to see if it stuck.

"Dude, come on!" Bright said, turning around and walking backward so he could see Ephram. "Don't you get it? She's signaling the pitch."

Ephram paused. "Please don't use sports metaphors right now. I need to understand what you're saying."

Bright rolled his eyes. "Women don't speak English," he said. "They speak in code. You've gotta translate to understand them. Madison can't just come out and say, 'Hey, come over on Friday and do me.'"

"For many reasons," Ephram said, marveling as always at Bright's unabashed crudeness.

"So she talks in code," Bright continued. "Like, if a girl says, 'Do you like this sweater?' what she means is 'Tell me how good I look.' And if Madison says, 'We can hang out without interruptions,' what she means is 'You might wanna stop at the drug-store on the way over.'"

Ephram took this in, let the nausea at the idea of condom-buying pass, and then considered it. He replayed his conversation with Madison over in his mind for the ten-thousandth time. Seen through

Bright's oversexed eyes, it did seem like she was sending him every signal in the book. Maybe he should go with his first instinct. Maybe he had been right from the beginning.

"She did say I should come over as soon as her roommate leaves. . . ."

"Hello?" Bright said, tipping his head back. "Does the little lassie need to hit you over the head with a heavy object here? She's achin' for some Brown lovin'. Dish it up and serve it hot, my friend."

Ew, Ephram thought. "Okay, okay," he said, swallowing hard. Then it hit him like a Manhattan crosstown bus. He was going to have sex. He was really going to have sex. "What should I do to prepare?" he asked.

"I don't know. Is there some special ritual you Jewish kids do, or do you just thank God and pray you don't screw it up like the rest of us?" Bright said.

Ephram raised his eyebrows. Yep. That was pretty much what he was going to be doing for the next twenty-four hours—that, and buying some condoms. . . .

"I'm going to need to come up with a really good story for my dad," Ephram said, trying to distract himself from the thought of browsing the Trojan section of the drugstore.

"Tell him you're hanging out at my house,"

Bright said with a shrug. "I'll cover for ya, dude."

"Yeah?"

Bright fake sniffled and wiped a phantom tear from his eye. "Our little Ephram's becoming a man."

"Thanks a lot," Ephram said, brushing by Bright.

"No worries!" Bright called after him. "But I'll be expecting a play-by-play!"

Friday night seemed like it would never come, but it did. And somehow, miraculously, Ephram was prepared. He had his poker-night-with-the-guys cover story all set and Bright was at home, ready to answer the phone and tell Ephram's dad that he was out grabbing the party grub. He had ironed his one cool button-down shirt, spent extra time gelling his hair, and had tucked a few condoms into the inside pocket of his black jacket. His heart may have been trying to pound its way out of his chest, but he looked cool. He looked the part. He looked like a guy who was about to have sex.

Just be cool, he told himself as he walked up the path to Madison's front door. *Take it slow. Act like a man. Be . . . cool.*

He rang the bell and put his hands in his pockets. No. Too "eager schoolboy." He hung his hands at his sides. Great. Now he looked like an ape. Oh, God, he was starting to sweat.

Okay, she's coming, Ephram thought. *Do something. Do . . .* something!

Quickly he reached his arm up and rested in on the doorframe, leaning his weight that way. The door opened and there Ephram was, posed like a mack-daddy playboy. Madison didn't even seem to notice.

"I couldn't decide if we should order Chinese or pizza so I called both," she said, brandishing the cordless phone. "Five bucks says the Kung-Pao gets here first, though the pizza guy does have that souped-up Camaro." She paused in her babbling and looked him up and down. "You look nice," she said with a smile.

Aw . . . yeah. It's on, Ephram thought, then almost laughed at himself. He had definitely been hanging out with Bright too much.

"So do you," he said, even though Madison was wearing her usual outfit of jeans and a T-shirt. She obviously hadn't dressed up for the occasion like Ephram had, but then, this was no big deal to her, right? Of course. People who had actually done it before didn't go all out. But Ephram wasn't lying. She did look amazing. She always looked amazing.

Madison smiled at his compliment, then turned and led him into the house. "The good news is I blew my Music Theory paper," she said, tossing the phone on a living room chair. She dropped onto the couch, crossed her legs, and looked up at him. "Better news is, now I have a makeup essay to write."

She was just making small talk. Being cool. But Ephram was more than ready to get this thing going.

"I think I know how to make you feel better," he said.

He leaned in and kissed her. He kissed her like they do it in the movies—hand behind her neck, hard and passionate, pressing her back into the couch. If he was going to do this, he was going to do it right.

But Madison pulled away quickly. "Hang on a sec," she said.

"Was that bad?" Ephram asked, caught off guard.

"No, I'm just sitting on a book," Madison said. She pulled out the textbook and dropped it on the floor and Ephram smiled and moved in for the kiss again. He felt Madison's lips tense up and she pulled away again, sliding down the couch.

"What's up with the mashing?" she asked, her brow creased.

Oh, God. I'm doing this all wrong, aren't I?

"I'm just a little nervous," Ephram explained, going for brutal honesty. "I don't want to mess this up."

"Mess what up?" Madison asked.

"It's just, I've never been here before. You have. I'm here now, which I'm grateful for, I might add," Ephram babbled. So much for playing it cool. "It's just . . . I don't know exactly what I'm doing."

"Neither do I," Madison said.

Ephram really looked at her for the first time. She looked thoroughly confused. Baffled, even.

Oh, God, he thought. *Oh, dear God, no.*

He was going to kill Bright. The only question was whether he was going to do it before or after he killed himself. How could he be so stupid?

"Oh my God," Madison said with a laugh. "Did you think we were having sex tonight?"

"No. No, I didn't," he said quickly. "Of course not."

Madison leaned back on the couch and crossed her arms over her chest, eyeing him. In his mind Ephram heard the words he had said moments ago. Yeah. It was pretty clear he thought they were having sex. Time to go on the defensive.

"Well, you said to come over because your roommate was out of town and . . . I thought . . . I mean, everybody knows what that means," Ephram said.

"Not *everyone*," Madison replied. "I don't know where you're getting your information, but when I say my roommate's going out of town, I mean my roommate is going out of town. Period."

Ephram's face was turning ten shades of red. He

had been right. She didn't want to have sex with him. Of course she didn't. How could he have been such a moron?

"New information," he said. "Glad to have it."

Madison let out a sigh. "Ephram, deciding to have sex is kind of a big deal."

"Even for you?" Ephram asked.

"Of course for me!" Madison said, standing up. "What do you think I am?!"

"I don't know!" Ephram replied, surprised at how upset she seemed. He stood up as well, the better to plead his case. "I thought it was only a big deal for first-timers. After you do it once, I figured it'd be just an extension of your average make-out session."

"Okay, you're officially not allowed to hang out with Bright anymore," Madison said.

Agreed, Ephram thought.

"The whole reason we work is because you don't think like that," she added, her expression softening. "Like a *guy* guy."

"So now I'm not even a guy?" Ephram said. "Sweet."

"No. You're better," she said, stepping closer to him. "It's a good thing. Trust me."

This time Ephram flushed for a whole other reason. Inside he was still miserable over his mistake and his disappointment, but a comment like that made him feel a bit better. Madison slid her arms around his neck and kissed him, and he felt better still.

Maybe all wasn't lost. This was a romantic moment. Maybe he could still convince her. And they *were* still alone . . .

Ephram deepened the kiss, pressing his fingertips into her back. Yeah. This was good. This was—

Madison pulled away. "You're trying again."

Ephram blinked. "No! No! You said we should talk. We were talking. . . ."

"Okay, that's it, cowboy." Madison said, smacking his chest with both hands and forcing him backward. "Time to go."

"What?" Ephram asked. She had to be joking.

"You're leaving," she said, turning him toward the door.

"But I was just—"

"And now you're done," she said.

"Can't I please just—"

She was pushing him toward the door and Ephram was struggling to find the words that would keep her from opening it. This couldn't be happening. Even if they didn't do *anything,* he had to stay here. He had nothing else to do tonight. And Madison had ordered food. . . . Where had it all gone wrong?

"No, you can't," she said, grabbing his jacket and handing it to him. Ephram looked at it like it was an alien object. He didn't even remember taking it off.

Madison opened the door and Ephram tripped out. Standing on the front step, jacket in hand, he felt like a little kid begging to be let into a party. This was not how this night was supposed to go.

"But could I just spend the night? I already asked my dad and—"

"You're done," Madison said again.

This time, Ephram got the message. Heart heavy, he turned around before she could close the door in his face. As he walked over to his car, all he could think about was how very wrong this was. He was supposed to be going home in the morning. He was supposed to be going home a non-virgin. He was supposed to be going home a man.

Unfortunately, he had never felt so much like a boy in his life.

If there was one thing this whole relationship situation was helping Ephram with, it was his apologies. He was becoming quite the accomplished apology-maker. And with each successive apology he was getting more creative, more whimsical, more sincere. At this rate he may be able to cultivate a career as a PR agent for one of those really awful celebrities—one of those people who were messing up all the time and needed to issue public statements explaining their actions. If the piano thing didn't work out, that was definitely another option.

Of course the difference was that in this case,

Ephram really *was* sorry—sorry for insulting Madison, for putting the moves on her, for making a fool of himself. He was pretty sure those celebrity types were never really sorry.

He rang the bell at her house. When she opened the door, she eyed him warily.

"You don't want to slam that," he told her. "If you do, I'll just park here outside your door and wait as long as it takes. You'll come out in the morning to get the paper and I'll be out here. Shivering. I brought a pillow and I'm not afraid to use it," he said, showing her the throw pillow he had hidden behind his back.

Madison cracked a small smile. "I hate when you have props."

Ephram returned the smile and then she opened the door a bit wider and tilted her head inside, telling him to follow her. This was why she hated props. They always seemed to do the trick.

"You have to know, when you get like that it makes me think you're not ready . . . for any of this," Madison said as they walked inside. "Sex isn't just having the place to yourself."

"I know," Ephram said.

"No, you don't. I don't know why sex is so complicated, but it is. It's something I have to talk about *before* it happens, not during," Madison said as she sat down on the couch. "And then there's you. One way or another you're going to remember your first time . . . for being wonderful or for being a disaster."

Ephram sat down next to her. "Which was it for you?" he asked, not sure he wanted to know.

Madison lifted her foot up onto the couch and pulled up the cuff of her jeans. Just above her ankle there was a small, U-shaped scar.

"You got *scarred*?" he asked.

"Alex Braco," Madison said with a small smile, tucking her foot under her. "We went to Camp Lenapee together for ten years, from when we were campers who held hands to the counselors who'd lock themselves in the boathouse during free swim," she said, turning on the couch to face him. "Our last summer Alex told me he was waiting till he was in love to have sex . . . and that he was in love with me."

"Nice one," Ephram said sarcastically. It was such an obvious line. But Madison's face fell slightly, like even though she knew it was a line too, it still upset her to hear it. Ephram resolved to keep his mouth shut and let her talk.

"Anyway, we met that night in the woods behind the tennis courts. He brought this thin sheet for us to lay on. It was so thin that I could feel every rock and twig beneath us," she said, then pointed to her scar again. "This was a sharp branch."

"Ouch," Ephram said, his heart starting to go out to her.

"The whole thing was crazy. I just remember being excited before he came to pick me up. My girlfriends were with me, helping me pick out what to wear. It all seemed so surreal," Madison said, looking off to the left slightly, like she didn't want to meet his eye. "And then I was there, and it was happening, and . . . it was scary and uncomfortable. Not just physically, but it was like suddenly everything was different except me. I didn't feel different enough for that to be happening to me," she said, her face growing more and more sorrowful as she talked. "And that's exactly how it felt, like it was happening *to* me and I was watching it from someplace else—not actually being a part of it."

By this point Madison looked thoroughly depressed, like she was back there, lying behind some tennis court in the middle of nowhere with some guy who didn't give a crap about her.

"Finally I just wanted it to be over, and it was."

"That doesn't sound very nice," Ephram said, wanting more than anything to hug her.

"Yeah. It's funny," Madison said flatly. "I haven't thought about that night in a long time."

"Is it weird to say that I wish I was there?" Ephram asked. "Not in a freaky 'I like to watch' kind of way," he said, earning a laugh from Madison. "But I can't stand the thought of you being unhappy—even in the past."

Madison looked at him like she'd never seen him

before. Her eyes were soft and she seemed . . . touched. She leaned forward and kissed him gently.

"You know what?" she said, her face inches from his.

"What?" Ephram asked.

"My roommate is still out of town."

Ephram's heart warmed with excitement. He knew he wasn't reading *that* wrong. He smiled and she kissed him again. And this time *he* wasn't the one doing the mashing.

Before long Ephram found himself on his back on the couch, shirt off, Madison on top of him in a tank top and jeans, a blanket wrapped around their waists. He wasn't cold, but he couldn't seem to make himself stop shivering. Apparently that was what happened to him at the pinnacle of nervous excitement: He shook like a leaf.

Madison kissed him passionately. Ephram tried to move his right arm, which was all pins and needles what with them both laying on it, but it was pinned between his body and the back of the couch. He did his best to concentrate on kissing and using his left hand to brush back Madison's hair, but the pins and needles grew more and more intense and the arm wouldn't move no matter how hard he tried. He was going to have to say something.

"I don't know what to do with my arm."

"Just leave it there," Madison said, kissing his neck.

"No, no. It's asleep," he said.

Madison giggled and Ephram laughed.

"Here," she said. She reached over, pulled his arm out and placed it across the small of her back. It was like a useless slab of meat, but at least the feeling was starting to come back.

"There you go. Much better," Ephram said.

They kissed again and Ephram shifted his legs, knocking over a lamp in the process. Very suave. Fortunately Madison didn't even seem to notice. She was actually very in to this.

Okay, do something. You can't let her do every-thing, Ephram told himself.

He reached down to the buckle on her belt, hardly able to believe he was really doing this. He fiddled with it, pulled at it, yanked at it. Nothing happened. Was he so inept that he couldn't even handle a belt? What was he going to do when it came time to deal with the bra?

"Having a little trouble here," he said, figuring she was about to notice his fumbling fingers anyway.

"Sorry. Weird belt," she said, lifting herself up a few inches. "I got it."

She reached down and undid the latch with one swift motion, then pulled the blanket up to cover their shoulders. Ephram relished the warmth. For a split second the shivering subsided. They kissed again and Ephram held her close. He was more than ready to do this thing, and he could tell Madison was too.

She actually wanted him. Could life be any more perfect?

"Did you buy condoms?" Madison asked, pulling back for a second.

Ephram's heart responded with an excited leap. "Yeah. In my bag."

Madison reached over Ephram's head to try to reach his bag and in the process her whole body pressed into his. When she couldn't quite reach, she pressed into him again. And again. And again.

Suddenly Ephram realized this was not good. Partially because it felt just *way too* good. He was already *so* ready to be with her and now she was . . . well . . . she was . . . she . . .

Oh, crap.

Ephram closed his eyes, mortified. That hadn't just happened. Madison came back into view with the condoms, ready to get to the next step. She had no idea that Ephram had already gotten there and come back down. The condoms would not be needed.

Madison was pulling out one of the little foil squares when Ephram sat up straight, clutching the blanket against his chest. This was not happening. This was so . . . *so* not happening.

"Are you okay?" Madison asked, her face all flushed, her hair all tousled.

"I . . . I can't do this now," Ephram said. It was the only thing he could think to say.

"Don't worry. We'll take it slow," Madison said.

"No." Ephram said, holding the blanket to him. "I *can't* do *this* . . . *now*."

He could cry. Seriously. He could really, *really* cry.

Madison looked at him and realization dawned on her face. Her eyes traveled down.

"Did you just—"

And then, she almost laughed. She was quick enough not to let it all the way out, but the damage was already done. Ephram wanted to die.

"It's not funny!" he said.

"Of course not," Madison said quickly. "I don't care. I don't care. It's fine."

"I care!" Ephram said.

Oh, God. Get me out of here. Get me out of here now. He couldn't stand the way she was looking at him. All pitying but trying not to look pitying. She must have thought he was such an inept little kid, so totally unworthy of all of this.

"Sweetie—"

"I gotta go."

Ephram jumped up, grabbed his shirt and sneakers, and was out the door before he had any of them on. As he raced to his car, his humiliation acting as an effective heat barrier against the cold, Ephram realized with horror that Madison was right. He *was* going to remember his first time forever—and not for being wonderful or horrible—but for not happening at all.

Twenty minutes later Ephram stormed into his house, wondering why the world hated him so much. Why couldn't anything good ever happen for him? Was it some kind of cosmic conspiracy? He couldn't help but feel that somewhere out there, someone was laughing at him.

He slammed the door, nothing on his mind but a shower and a nice long night of playing the worst moment of his life over and over and over again in his mind until he went insane.

"Well, it's about time," his father said sternly, greeting him at the door.

"Not now," Ephram said, blowing right by him.

"'Not now'? Try *right* now," his father said, following him into the kitchen where, just to make things worse, Delia and Linda were making cookies. "Wanna tell me again about last night's poker game? 'Cause I had a very interesting conversation with Dr. Abbott today. . . ."

Ephram paused. This was ridiculous. So the lie he'd told last night so that he could have sex with Madison had been uncovered. Who cared? Nothing had happened then. Nothing had happened tonight. Nothing was going to happen ever.

"Fine! I made it up!" he said, reeling on his father. "But I came home anyway, so I don't see what the big deal is."

"You lied. That's what the big deal is," his father said.

Linda and Delia looked at each other and quickly slipped out of the room. Ephram would have given ten million dollars to go with them.

"Ground me and get it over with," he told his father. "Because I'm not in the mood—"

"You better get in the mood!" his father shouted. "Because we are going to have a conversation about this. And by conversation I mean *you* are going to talk to me about what the hell is going on in your life. Starting right now. Where were you tonight?"

Ephram stared down at the top of the island in the kitchen. *I was embarrassing myself to the full extent of possibility,* he thought.

"Out," he said.

"Not good enough."

"I was at Madison's," Ephram said.

"Are you sleeping with her?"

Ephram laughed. Could his father's timing *be* any more ironic?

"Answer me!" his father said.

"No! All right? I'm not sleeping with her!" Ephram exploded, all the pent up emotion spewing out of him. "I'll probably never sleep with her or anyone else, for that matter. I'm gonna die a virgin because that's just how my life is. Anything good that happens to me goes bad and anything bad that happens to me gets worse whenever humanly possible. Does that make you happy? Is that what you wanted to hear?"

The expression on his dad's face shifted from pure ire to concern in two seconds. "What happened?" he asked.

"Can I please go now?" Ephram asked, desperate to be alone.

Finally his father nodded and Ephram ran upstairs, taking the steps two at a time. But even up in his room, where he usually felt safe, he realized there was no escape. His worst nightmare had been realized and there was nothing he could do to take it back.

He dropped down on the edge of his bed and pressed the heels of his hands into his eyes, wishing he could do away with the mental image of Madison's face when she had realized what had happened. But it was never going to go away. Madison may have walked away from her encounter at Camp Lenapee with a scar on her ankle, but Ephram's was going to be much worse.

His pride was scarred for life.

The next day Ephram and his father were having their traditional post-fight talk when Delia and Madison returned from the movies. Just one look at Madison and Ephram wanted to crawl under a rock somewhere and hide. He wasn't sure if he was ever going to be able to look her in the eye again. She probably didn't even want him to.

"Hey, Dr. Brown," Madison said, then looked at Ephram quickly.

Delia ran upstairs and Madison just sort of hovered near the door.

I knew it. She wants nothing to do with me, Ephram thought.

"Come on in," his father said to Madison.

"Actually, you wanna go out for a little bit?" Madison asked Ephram.

His stomach lurched. "Yeah . . . ," he said uncertainly. "Sure." Then he looked at his dad, just praying he wouldn't make the situation worse by saying no.

"Have fun," his father said.

Ephram grabbed his jacket and headed out with Madison, unsure of what was going to happen next. Was she going to break up with him? Was she going to give him the "It happens to every guy" speech? What?

A little while later, after a fairly silent car ride, Ephram and Madison were looking out the windshield of Ephram's car at the Point. It was ironic that this was where they had ended up, considering making out was pretty much the last thing on Ephram's mind. He wasn't sure he ever wanted to go there again.

He looked at Madison. She looked at him. They both smiled awkwardly then looked away. Some-one had to say something. Ephram took a deep breath.

"So, I thought of a bright side," he said.

"Oh yeah?" Madison sounded doubtful and hopeful all at once.

"Mm-hmm," Ephram said. "The condom didn't have a chance to break."

Madison laughed and Ephram smiled. Some of his tension was relieved.

"You know what we need?" Madison asked.

"I still miss my pride," Ephram joked, on a roll.

Madison rolled her eyes, still grinning. "We need a song."

"I already wrote you a song. Didn't work out so good either, remember?"

"A radio song, dumbass," Madison said. "So whenever you hear it you get a goofy grin and go, 'Oh, that's our song,' and people can make fun of you."

Ephram smiled. She was trying to lighten the situation. To get back to where they had been before all the heinous sex-capades. And she wanted to have a song with him. It was actually kind of sweet.

"Only problem is, we never agree on music," Ephram said.

"Fine. I'm turning on the radio. Whatever's on,

that's it," Madison said, her eyes bright. "You in?"

"We could end up with a shaving jingle," Ephram pointed out.

Madison reached over and turned the knob on the old-fashioned radio. A country-western voice crooned from the speakers.

"I'd climb the highest mountain . . ."

Madison and Ephram cracked up laughing.

"Okay, bad idea," Madison said.

"Come on. It's a perfect anthem for youthful misguided longing," Ephram said.

"Best two out of three?" Madison suggested, raising her eyebrows.

She hit another button, changing the station on the radio, and out blasted some serious seventies disco. Total cheese. Ephram laughed again.

"One more time," she said.

"Give it up!" he told her, laughing.

"Never!"

Something about her total determination to do this made Ephram's heart skip over and over again. He grabbed her hand before it could reach the radio and stopped her with a kiss. A real, serious kiss.

Madison stopped reaching for the radio and slipped her arms around him. Ephram cradled her face with his hands. This wasn't about getting the deed done or wondering whether he was doing it right. This was about Madison and how beautiful and perfect and amazing and funny and caring and understanding she was. All he wanted in the world was to be with her. And as soon as he realized that, it was all too easy.

Madison pulled away from him, her breath heavy, and one look in her eyes told Ephram she was thinking the same thing. She slipped out of her jacket, then helped him out of his. Before Ephram knew it, the moment had come. It was all happening—the moment he *would* remember for the rest of his life.

Him and Madison. In his big boat of a car at the Point. Holding each other, kissing each other, giggling, smiling, and loving every minute of it.

Ephram knew his world would never be the same. And he didn't mind one bit.

As many as 1 in 3 Americans
who have HIV...don't know it.

TAKE CONTROL.
KNOW YOUR STATUS.
GET TESTED.

To learn more about HIV testing,
or get a free guide to HIV and
other sexually transmitted diseases:

www.knowhivaids.org
1-866-344-KNOW

EVERWOOD

Ephram Brown has a pretty good life in New York City—great friends, a gift for playing the piano, and a really cool mom. The only thing he doesn't have is the best relationship with his dad, famous neurosurgeon Dr. Andy Brown. How could he, when the Great Dr. Brown is too busy saving lives to spend any time with him?

Then Ephram's mom dies suddenly in a car accident. And as if things couldn't get any worse, his father loses his mind and decides to move the family to a tiny town in Colorado called Everwood.

In Everwood their new lives begin. . . .

Look for a new Everwood novel every other month!

PUBLISHED BY SIMON & SCHUSTER